Martin Millar was born and brought up in Glasgow. He moved to south London and became a young punk rocker. He is the author of *Milk, Sulphate and Alby Starvation, Lux the Poet, Ruby and the Stone Age Diet, The Good Fairies of New York* and *Dreams of Sex and Stage-Diving*.

Jamie Hewlett and Alan Martin, the creators of *Tank Girl*, met at Worthing Art College. There they broke new ground in the world of graphic novels with their homemade fanzine *Atomtan*. The partnership progressed and Tank Girl was born; she was an immediate and startling success. Both Jamie Hewlett and Alan Martin now live in Worthing.

TANK GIRL: THE MOVIE

A NOVEL BY MARTIN MILLAR

BASED UPON THE MOTION PICTURE
WRITTEN BY TEDI SARAFIAN
BASED UPON THE COMIC STRIP CREATED BY
ALAN MARTIN AND JAMIE HEWLETT

PENGUIN BOOKS

PENGUIN BOOKS

Published by the Penguin Group
Penguin Books Ltd, 27 Wrights Lane, London w8 5tz, England
Penguin Books USA Inc., 375 Hudson Street, New York, New York 10014, USA
Penguin Books Australia Ltd, Ringwood, Victoria, Australia
Penguin Books Canada Ltd, 10 Alcorn Avenue, Toronto, Ontario, Canada m4v 3b2
Penguin Books (NZ) Ltd, 182–190 Wairau Road, Auckland 10, New Zealand

Penguin Books Ltd, Registered Offices: Harmondsworth, Middlesex, England

First published by Penguin Books 1995
1 3 5 7 9 10 8 6 4 2

Set in 10/13pt Monophoto Times by
Datix International Ltd, Bungay, Suffolk
Printed in England by Clays Ltd, St Ives plc

I

I do not like Tank Girl. Let me rephrase that: I detest Tank Girl. She is a braggart, a loud-mouth, a bully, a show-off, a cheat, a liar, a boor, a drunk, a fool, a thief; she wears terrible clothes, she has a ridiculous hairstyle, she doesn't pay her debts, she has no culture and no good conversation. Even among the lowlife clientele of Big Mary's Bar and Grill, she stands out as a notable example of detestableness.

'Your round, Tank Girl.'

'No I'm not, I'm long and skinny.'

Tank Girl is in paroxysms of laughter at her feeble joke. I hate her. In her customary arrogant manner, she sends Jet Girl off to the bar to pick up a trayful of beer.

Every year in the Wastelands it rains continuously for forty days and forty nights. Somewhere around day thirty-six the Annual Wastelands Snap and Drinking Competition gets under way at Big Mary's Bar and Grill, which is why I am now sitting at this filthy table surrounded by glasses of beer and piles of money. Around the table are my fellow players – some human, some kangaroo and some unconscious. One of those still conscious is, unfortunately, Tank Girl. At the end of every hand of snap each participant, apart from the winner, has to down a large glass of beer. Around the table are the prostrate bodies of those who have collapsed from the effects of twenty-four hours' drinking. Anyone who collapses forfeits their stake to the table. Personally, I refuse to collapse, and though there are many better things I could be doing with my time, I refuse to lose to Tank Girl either at snap or at drinking.

We drink. Jet Girl, sitting beside Tank Girl, looks somewhat unsteady on her chair, but manages to stay awake.

'Had enough?' asks Tank Girl, flashing her large, malicious smile.

'Deal the cards, Tank Girl,' I reply.

She frowns; then pouts. Why she pouts, I don't know. It looks ridiculous. She shuffles the cards and looks over at me.

'Did I ever tell you about the time I saved the world?'

2

Tank Girl fumbles with the pack. I watch her like a hawk, because I know she is trying to cheat.

'Did I ever tell you about the time I saved the world?' she repeats.

'Yes, you did. Deal the cards.'

'It was some time after the great comet struck the earth,' she continues, despite the fact that neither I nor anyone else around the table want to hear the story. Even her damned kangaroo companions are bored with it. But among Tank Girl's many detestable character traits is an overwhelming urge to tell stories about herself. Where she gets these outlandish stories from is a mystery to me, because I'm sure she doesn't have the intelligence to make them up. Perhaps Sub Girl makes them up for her. Sub Girl is at least rumoured to be intelligent. She's also a pain, though not as bad as Tank Girl.

And Tank Girl begins to ramble on about the calamity that shook the earth back in the old days. I know why she's doing it: she wishes to break everyone's concentration on the game. With her propensity for cheating and her crude diversionary tactics, Tank Girl makes a terrible opponent.

'Deal the cards, Tank Girl,' says Mining Jim, who is sitting on my left.

'In a minute. I was just telling you about the time the comet struck the earth . . .'

One of her kangaroo friends suddenly throws up over

himself and falls off his chair. Tank Girl, Sub Girl and Jet Girl laugh till the tears flow down their faces.

'Ha ha,' chortles Tank Girl. 'Poor old T-Saint never could hold his drink. Gather in his money.'

It is common knowledge around the Wastelands that Tank Girl sleeps with one of these kangaroos. Disgusting, or what? A grey fog suddenly envelops my head as the effects of twenty-four hours' drinking catch up with me. I shake my head vigorously to clear it. I may be only a humble trader in late-'seventies antiques, but I'm damned if I'm going to lose a drinking contest to a woman who sleeps with a kangaroo.

Outside, the rain pours down. It is day thirty-seven of the rains. Three more to go. The weather was never like this in my old 'seventies videos. Three-hundred-and-twenty-five days of burning sunshine, which bakes the desert hard, dry and dead, followed by forty days and forty nights of rain. At least it's consistent.

Big Mary wanders up, kicks the fallen kangaroo out of the way and gathers up the glasses. She has muscular arms, long black hair and what looks like an old Colt revolver tucked in her apron. Big Mary doesn't like any trouble in her bar.

'Yes,' says Tank Girl, 'when the great comet struck I was only a little girl, can't have been more than four or five. I was precociously intelligent and brave even then, of course, always having adventures and stuff. I remember, I crossed the desert on my tricycle, can't have been more than three or four at the time. My parents were frantic –'

'No doubt in case you were rescued. Deal the cards, Tank Girl.'

Tank Girl's eyes narrow, rather threateningly.

4

'Do I sense a slight hostility on your part, Trader?'

I don't answer, but, not for the first time, I wish guns weren't banned from Big Mary's during the Annual Wastelands Snap and Drinking Competition (apart from those carried by the bar-staff, of course). Everyone entering Big Mary's has to either leave their gun outside or check it in with the doormen. I have a reasonably modern plasma rifle outside in the Big Trader Truck and am fairly proficient in its use – you don't succeed as a 'seventies antique dealer in the Wastelands without learning how to look after yourself. Many's the time I've been bushwhacked by gangs of ten or more armed robbers intent on stealing my cargo of *Blake's Seven* and *Tomorrow People* videos, but they've never got the better of me. I'm no pushover.

'The Trader's no pushover,' as they say in the Wastelands. Although, to be absolutely honest, I'm only no pushover with my plasma rifle in my hand. Unarmed, Tank Girl would tear me apart.

I am on my own here. Tank Girl is accompanied by Jet Girl, Sub Girl and several strong kangaroos. Outside, they have a tank, a submarine and a jet, which made finding a parking space for the Big Trader Truck something of a problem. I guess it would be unwise to offend Tank Girl too much.

It strikes me that, even if I win the contest, it may not be easy to make a clean getaway with the prize money. Tank Girl is not the sort of person to honour agreements.

She picks at the sticking plaster on her forehead. She's been letting on that she had a little trouble with some government soldiers on the way here, but, really, all that happened was that she fell over and banged her head when she was drunk. I know this for a fact. A kangaroo told me.

'Yep, that old comet certainly changed things around here,' continues Tank Girl.

'It certainly did,' agrees Jet Girl. 'Remember Kesslee?'

'Do I remember Kesslee? I certainly do. Now, was he a swine or not?'

'The worst,' says Sub Girl.

'Appalling,' agrees Booga, who, I understand, is Tank Girl's favourite kangaroo. Or Genetically Engineered Super Soldier, as the kangaroos would have it, though if 'No Brain' Booga is a Genetically Engineered Super Soldier, then I'm Santa Claus.

'. . . So, although the comet more or less wiped out civilization as we knew it, turning the continent into a barren wasteland, altering the weather, throwing up new mountain ranges and making beer really hard to come by, I wasn't too badly off, even though I was only five at the time. I knew how to look after myself and, when the gangs started to roam around in the chaos, I just took to the desert and survived in the wilds.'

'Of course –' she glances out of the window at the ceaseless downpour – 'there wasn't even any rain then, so most people just died of thirst in the first couple of years. I survived by drinking milk from coconuts and stuff like that, no problem really for a woman of my capabilities, then I fell in with a bunch of hippies and lived with them for a while, which was okay –'

I grit my teeth. If this drunken woman thinks she's going to put me off my cards with this sort of rambling, she's much mistaken, but there is no stopping her. She loves the sound of her own voice too much. She dips one of her plaits into her beer, then sticks it in her mouth and carries on with her life story.

The cards are dealt and we start to go round.

To tell you the truth, I am now feeling a little nervous. Tank Girl likes me no better than I like her and she's eyeing my pot of money greedily. I would say that, if I am the ultimate winner of the Annual Wastelands Snap and Drinking Competition, then there is little chance of me walking out of here with my winnings.

I have one thing in my favour. Prior to coming here I had the Big Trader Truck secretly supercharged at O'Halleran's garage, just down from the Red Mountains. The Big Trader Truck, generally an object of ridicule and derision throughout the Wastelands, because of its inability to climb a slight incline at more than five miles an hour, is now the proud bearer of a brand-new XTF 98 engine. What exactly 'XTF 98' means, I have no idea, but it goes pretty damn fast. If I do have to make a rapid getaway, as long as I can actually make it to the vehicle, I'll be safe. Wasteland inhabitants, used to having a good laugh at the sight of the Big Trader Truck lumbering painfully over the dunes, will gape in wonder as I roar off like a bolt of lightning.

Of course, this would depend on me actually making it out of Big Mary's Bar and Grill in the first place. After twenty-five hours' continuous drinking I might well find it difficult to walk that far. No one would stop Tank Girl and her accomplices from robbing me. So, I'm just starting to think that things are looking very bad for me indeed, when, to my great relief, the door to Big Mary's flies open and in come the Wasteland Ninjas.

'Shut that damned door,' shouts Big Mary, as the

wind and rain pour through. Ten or so Wasteland Ninjas file into the Bar and Grill, water glistening on their short blue hair and dripping from their black cloaks.

Tank Girl curses out loud.

'Not those Ninja weirdos,' she growls. 'Who asked them here? They don't play cards.'

'Don't drink either,' says Jet Girl.

Indeed they don't. All they do is wander about the desert practising survival skills and the ancient fighting arts, and this is very good news for me, because the Wasteland Ninjas are my allies. More than that, they positively love me, because I am the only man on the continent who can provide them with fresh supplies of their Holy Relic: videos of the ancient and revered *Kung Fu* TV series, starring the equally ancient and revered David Carradine.

Eldrich San, their leader, dispatches a minion to the bar for glasses of water or carrot juice or whatever disgusting thing it is they drink, and I hear Big Mary grumbling about the inconvenience of it all.

Eldrich San approaches the table.

'Greetings.'

'Bug off, freak-face,' says Tank Girl.

Eldrich San ignores this, as befits a top-grade Ninja warrior, and turns to me.

'You have brought us videos to trade?'

'Absolutely,' I say, and rather drunkenly clap him on the shoulder. He withdraws slightly, because the head of the Wasteland Ninjas does not really enjoy being clapped on the shoulder. Quite a social gaffe in fact, but never mind.

'Yes, I have located numbers three, eight and nine of

the second series, as requested. They're over there in that bag beside the statue.'

During my last mission seeking antiques in the desert I dug up an old statue of a woman. It's not worth anything, but I rather like it and have propped it on a seat in the corner, where someone has decorated it with a baseball cap and lipstick.

'I'm busy playing cards just now, but feel free to peruse them and I'll be happy to negotiate their sale as soon as I've cleaned out my opponents in the Annual Wastelands Snap and Drinking Competition.'

Eldrich San nods, gathers his soggy robes about him and goes back to his companions, who are gathered around the pinball machine. I'm pleased to see that Ootsie and Bitsy, two young recruits to the Wasteland Ninjas, are in the group, as they are friends of mine and owe me some favours.

Around the table there is silence, and I see that Tank Girl is herself re-evaluating the balance of forces.

Sub Girl, across the table from me, plays the eight of spades, and I whack down the eight of clubs.

'*Snap!*' I scream in triumph, and gather in the pot of money in front of me. 'Another victory for the Trader!'

There is a murmur of appreciation from the watching audience.

'Sub Girl, you doom-brain, why did you play that?' demands Tank Girl, to which the Mystic Prophetess and Underground Queen of the Submarines can only shrug her shoulders.

The glasses are filled and everybody has to drink except me, as I won the last hand. Jet Girl looks distinctly queasy, but Tank Girl drinks with apparent gusto. And Tank Girl, damn her, will not shut up.

3

Tank Girl claims that it was thanks to her that the old days came to an end, but Tank Girl is a notorious liar.

She is telling us about her time in the hippy commune. I wish she wouldn't. For one thing, her voice irritates me, and for another, I do not much like thinking about the old days, because the old days were terrible.

She spits on the table.

'Of course, by this time things had got pretty bad. After the comet struck, that is. Just desert everywhere, and the little water there was under the control of Water and Power, which, you may remember, was itself controlled by that total creep Kesslee, number one asshole in the known universe. So, more or less everyone had to do what Water and Power said and everyone had to buy water from them or else die, and it was illegal to find your own water; in fact, it was illegal to do anything at all. Life was just one great big desert filled with Kesslee's soldiers, and Kesslee was running everything like a dictator, to the general distress of the suffering population. Pretty standard post-apocalyptic scenario in fact.

'But this hippy commune was tucked away in the Blue Dunes and they had their own secret well. Everything there was okay for a while, well, anyway, there was plenty of dope and I used to shag this guy called Richard who was all right except when he was lecturing me about being too stoned all the time to take my turn at communal cooking –'

Here she breaks off and laughs loudly at the very thought.

'I mean, can you imagine me making bowls of lentils for everyone? Completely ridiculous. Where was I?'

'You were about to play your card,' I say.

'I'll play when I'm ready,' says Tank Girl.

Last card played was the four of clubs, and Tank Girl is delaying placing her card on top. Which makes me think that she quite possibly knows she has a four and is waiting till everyone else is distracted before putting it down so she can call 'snap!' first and win the round.

Does everyone know how to play snap? It's the simplest game. The pack is dealt out face-down to all the players, so no one knows what card is going to be played next. Players take it in turn to play a card and, if two cards of the same denomination follow each other – for instance, if someone plays the eight of clubs on top of the eight of spades – then the first person to call 'snap!' and get their hand down on the pack wins the round. There is not a lot of skill involved. This competition is more about drinking and endurance. Still, you do have to win a round occasionally because, if you don't have enough money to put in your stake, then you are out of the game.

So, no one is meant to know what card they are going to play next but, as Tank Girl has no morals, she is undoubtedly peeking. So am I.

'I met Little Wee Sam in the commune,' she goes on. Everyone looks down at Little Wee Sam, who is lying under the table in a pool of vomit, being rather too small to withstand twenty-five hours' drinking.

'Only ten at the time and a good artist, I seem to

11

remember. This was before she started drinking, of course.

'But one day . . .'

Tank Girl pauses, scratching her breasts.

'One day . . .'

The rain pounds against the window.

'One day . . .'

'What?'

'*Snap!*' screams Tank Girl, pounding down the four of hearts. 'Game to me!'

'You cheated!' I shout.

'Is that so?' yells Tank Girl, standing up and glaring defiantly at me.

I stand up, the kangaroos stand up, Jet Girl and Sub Girl stand up, Mining Jim and his mates stand up, the Wasteland Ninjas make a move towards us, chaos threatens, and for a second it seems the expected battle may erupt.

'Shut up and drink,' bawls Big Mary, smashing down a trayful of lager in front of us. 'I'll have no fighting in my bar.'

We sit down. Everyone has to drink except Tank Girl, who won. I detest her.

4

Tank Girl is braying about her small victory, the kangaroos are slapping her on the back, and I am forcing down what seems like my hundredth glass of beer when – curse them! – the Shaolin Queens of the Desert walk in. What a terrible stroke of luck. The Shaolin Queens of the Desert are another menace to society. They wear their hair in topknots dyed red, and black combat clothes studded with cheap jewels and mirror fragments, and march around the desert threatening to fight anyone they don't like the look of. I always get the feeling they don't like the look of me. What makes this particularly unfortunate though, is that the Shaolin Queens of the Desert are natural enemies of the Wasteland Ninjas and will side against them in any fight. As the Shaolin Queens spend half their lives practising their Shaolin Kung Fu, they are not a group whom one would wish to fight unnecessarily. The odds have again swung in Tank Girl's favour.

Tank Girl realizes this and sends Booga the stupid kangaroo over to buy them all a drink. Booga is himself suffering the effects of alcohol. Hopping haphazardly towards the bar he makes a pathetic sight.

Less ascetic than the Wasteland Ninjas, the Shaolin Queens proceed to make merry with three bottles of whisky and a small glass of water and come over to watch the game.

'Welcome, Shaolin Queens of the Desert,' bawls Tank Girl. 'Grab a chair and watch me clean up these suckers at cards. You're just in time for my story about how the soldiers from Water and Power brought an abrupt end to my days of paradisiacal hippy living in the commune.'

'Fire away,' says Magdalen, leader of the Shaolin Queens, swinging her legs over a stool and clearing a place at the table with her elbows. Magdalen is an out-and-out thug if ever I met one. 'Always enjoy a good story.'

Tank Girl, out of bravado, drinks down her beer, though, as winner of the last round, she is not obliged to.

'Drink up, Trader,' she says. 'You're falling behind.'

I drink: I feel ill. Tank Girl carries on with her story, which puts me off my play. The game goes round and I seem unable to win another hand. The pile of money in front of me starts to shrink. This is perturbing. Due to various business expenses, notably the purchase of the XTF 98 engine and a four-week binge at the end of my last trip, I did not arrive at Big Mary's with a great deal of money, although I do have various artefacts to sell. I try and concentrate. I will be furious if I am forced out of the game. Not only that, I'll be in deep trouble with ZugZug the Bookmaker.

'Yes, that hippy commune was a strange place for a woman like me,' continues Tank Girl. 'Plenty of dope but almost no excitement, unless you count the frequent arguments about whose turn it was to sweep the stairs and who ate all the peanut butter. As I never swept the stairs and continually ate the peanut butter, most of the arguments seemed to centre on me. I guess I'm just not suited to communal living, unless all the other people do whatever I want. Like Booga here, for instance. To

14

you he might just look like a pathetically deformed kangaroo, but to me he's the best tea-maker in the Wastelands. Run and make me a brew in the kitchen will you?'

Booga trots off.

'So for a bit of excitement, I used to go out in the desert and ride the buffalos.'

'Buffalos don't live in the desert,' says the Professor.

'The buffalos had adapted well to living in the desert,' says Tank Girl. 'They are very clever animals. I used to hide behind a rock, wait till one wandered by, then leap on its back, and off we'd go. Sometimes I'd take one home to the commune, but all the hippies would start moaning about "animal exploitation" and "poor buffalo" and suchlike. I kept telling them the buffalo loved it, but they never understood. So, I mainly stayed out in the desert, and that was how I came to win my first serious fight, and also how I became such an expert with guns.

'One day, I was riding along quite contentedly singing "Home, Home on the Range" and eating a jar of peanut butter with my fingers, when a Water and Power armoured patrol appeared on the horizon. The patrols hadn't been to our area for a while, so it took me by surprise. They spotted me and started coming my way. I was just going to turn and flee when, for the first time, my true Tank Girl nature came to the surface.

'"Why should I run away?" I thought. I've as much right to be here as they have. Anyway, the stupid damn buffalo wouldn't turn round. They were always quite hard to control. So I simply charged the patrol. Took them completely by surprise. There were two armoured

15

cars and a truck full of troops, and I could see them all staring at me in amazement as I raced towards them.

'"Watch out, there's a woman on a buffalo charging at us!" I heard one of them scream, and then I rammed right into the side of one of the armoured cars. It skidded into the other one, and they both lost control and rolled down the side of this really steep sand-dune.'

As she says this, Tank Girl rolls two glasses off the table, demonstrating how it happened. They smash on to the floor. I'd like to make some comment, but am lost for words. Here I am, sitting playing cards with a woman who claims to have destroyed two armoured cars armed only with a pet buffalo. Something must have gone wrong with my life somewhere.

'The soldiers spilled out of the truck. I whacked a few of them with my baseball bat and grabbed one of their guns. I'd never held a gun before but I took to it immediately. Most of them were dead before they got out of the truck, and the rest fled. Not particularly brave of them, but I suppose they were only expecting to come up against harmless hippies and starving peasants. Weren't prepared at all for the savage and ferocious Tank Girl laying into them with a baseball bat.

'I gathered up all the guns, fed the buffalo the contents of the soldiers' lunch-boxes and trotted off home.'

Tank Girl pauses, frowning.

'And you know what happened when I got there? The stupid hippies were annoyed about it. Morons! You might have thought they'd be pleased, what with me single-handedly destroying a patrol and bringing home a bundle of weapons, but no, all they did was moan that I'd draw attention to the area, and now

16

Water and Power would be out hunting the attackers. Just jealous, that was their problem.

'But that was my first real fight. Afterwards, I used to take the guns out into the desert and practise. I practised till I could hit a coconut at 3000 yards. Soon there wasn't a coconut left in the area. Look, why is everybody sitting around this table doing nothing? Are we playing cards or what?'

5

Tank Girl, her legs up on the table (she is quite unable to sit properly on a chair), tells her less than thrilling story about life in the commune, which seems mainly to involve her being stoned all the time and occasionally playing with her sex toys.

'Pretty damned dull, in fact, apart from my pet buffalo, which I used to ride around on when I was bored. Still, it livened up when the Water and Power soldiers attacked.'

'Why did they attack?' asks the sycophantic Booga.

'Just felt like it, I suppose. They were like that, these Water and Power soldiers, always attacking someone or other. Kept them busy, I suppose. The excuse they used was that we had an illegal well. Remember, their company was supposed to be in charge of all the water. Water was hard to find after the giant comet struck –'

'We've heard about the giant comet. Get to the point.'

'Okay, don't rush a girl. I had, if I remember correctly, just been to see Little Wee Sam, who was remarkably cute in those days –'

There is a brief pause while everybody glances at the still young but far from cute figure of Sam lying comatose under the table, a bottle of whisky cradled lovingly in her grubby arms.

'Sam was making me a sculpture. Doris Day, I think, or maybe Johnny Prophet. Anyway, after that I just nipped out into the desert, hoping to shag Richard –

who was nothing great, I have to admit, but had a bit more stamina than the rest of the hippies – when these soldiers appeared from nowhere and started shooting at everyone. Complete chaos. I mean we had a few guns stashed away, and I gave as good as I got, better, in fact, I was mowing them down like nobody's business. A soldier came at me with a bayonet. I grabbed it off him. "Eat this, pig face," I said, and rammed it into him. Soon there was a pile of bodies at my feet – I realized I was quite enjoying myself – but the rest of the hippies –'

She shrugs.

'Pretty hopeless, really. They were all dead in a few minutes.'

Tank Girl displays a noticeable absence of grief at this sad revelation. She is completely heartless. I hate her. Jet Girl is nice, though. In fact, the more I drink, the nicer Jet Girl seems. She is wearing this really attractive yellow headscarf . . . I digress.

'They captured me and threw me into a helicopter, although even then I killed a few more with my bare hands.'

She bursts out laughing, remembering fondly how one of the soldiers had tried to molest her in the helicopter, and she had contrived to send him plunging out of the door, to splatter on the ground below. She laughs so much she almost chokes, and Booga has to pour a little beer down her throat to get her talking again.

'So, after that they chained me up and stayed well away from me till we landed in the huge, vast, technologically advanced military industrial complex that was in those days the headquarters of Water and Power. There were soldiers everywhere, and groaning slaves being whipped to make them work faster. I could tell that the opportunities for fun in such a place were going to be minimal.

'They dragged me up in front of Kesslee, and I do not exaggerate when I say that Kesslee was the biggest creep that ever walked the earth or crawled upon it. Everywhere else on the continent was just desert, but he used to sit around in an office that had so much water in it it was like being in the middle of the ocean, and all these other creeps used to come in and go out with their heads bowed, like they were terrified of the guy.

'Kesslee was boss of Water and Power, which made him ruler of the continent. As soon as they took me inside I tripped over a plant and knocked over a fish-tank. A terrible scene. We tried to rescue the fish, but it was hopeless. Every time anyone took a step, they'd squash one underfoot. Soon there were mangled fish everywhere. Got us off to a terrible start, really.'

Just round from me at the table, I can see that the Professor is nodding off, bored no doubt by the tediousness of Tank Girl's story. Still, he's done well to last this long in the game, being more the sort of guy built for intellect than physical endurance. The Professor's still got a good pile of money in front of him, he's been winning enough hands of snap to keep going and he's drunk down as much beer as all the other players.

The Professor is very clever. I presume this is why he is called the Professor.

I rather like him. Only last week I sold him two ancient books: Thackeray's *Vanity Fair* and Goldsmith's *The Vicar of Wakefield*. Let him have them at a bargain price. Mind you it's a very small market these days, nineteenth-century literature. Well, to be honest, there probably wasn't anyone else on the whole continent who would have wanted to buy them. Anyway, he was pleased.

Just as he is about to nod off, Big Mary pounds down another round and the crash of the tray on the table jerks him upright. He sips his beer, shakes his head and makes an effort to stay awake.

Tank Girl is still droning on.

'Possibly the worst thing about Kesslee was that he used to quote poetry. Drove me to distraction. I mean, when you're lying manacled at some guy's feet and all your friends have just been shot, the last thing you want is somebody reciting poetry to you.'

'Perhaps he was trying to be comforting?' suggests the Professor. 'A nice poem can be very soothing in moments of crisis.'

'Please, Professor,' says Tank Girl, giving him a withering glance. 'If he'd wanted to comfort me, he'd have given me a cup of tea and a toasted muffin. He just liked the sound of his own voice. Much the same as me, I suppose.'

'So what did Kesslee do?' I ask, not because I am at all interested, just to move the story along so we can get back to playing cards.

'He asked me to work for him,' replies Tank Girl. 'The man recognized quality when he saw it. "Tank Girl", he said, "you killed forty-eight of my soldiers with an old rifle and your trusty baseball bat. An incredible performance. Water and Power needs you. Come and work for me and I'll make you mistress of all you survey." He went on like this for a while, offering me fabulous wealth and power until, eventually, I fell asleep. I think that's what got us off to such a bad start. That and the dead fish. We were never really friends after that.'

6

A disturbance breaks out behind us as some of the Shaolin Queens of the Desert get into an argument with the Wasteland Ninjas over who is next on the pool-table. As they are deadly enemies, it immediately threatens to turn violent and, as Big Mary hurries over to calm things down, I notice that she now has what appear to be *two* old Colt revolvers stuck in her apron. With the steam still rising off the Shaolin Queens' wet clothes and the general smog in the room after twenty-five hours of smoking, drinking and card-playing, it is a little difficult to see precisely what is happening, but, anyway, Magdalen, leader of the Shaolin Queens, is leaping over to see what the trouble is, and Eldrich San, the head Ninja, is up on his feet shouting that his name was the next one chalked up on the board.

I never knew Eldrich San was so keen on pool. It must be the influence of Ootsie and Bitsy, who, as I mentioned, are young recruits. Although they are both Wasteland Ninjas now and spend most of their time tramping over the desert, I can remember the days when they were never away from the pool-table. Pair of young hustlers, in fact. Most unsuitable material for the Ninjas, I would have thought.

Before the disturbance at the pool-table can develop into anything serious, everyone's attention is diverted by the door bursting open. The freezing rain and wind pour in again. Still audible over the noise of the storm is the sound of engines dying down.

'Big Mary, gimme a beer,' bawls the new arrival, stomping into the room, followed by eight or nine others. They're all dressed in shabby black leathers, big biker boots and full-scale Native American head-dresses made from buzzard feathers dyed green. Their faces are daubed with green warpaint and more buzzard feather jewelry hangs from their ears.

I rejoice. It's the Post-Apocalypse Biker Girls. They've come to watch the Annual Wastelands Snap and Drinking Competition. Now, the Post-Apocalypse Biker Girls are no particular friends of mine, though they are not enemies either, but the reason I rejoice is that they are sworn enemies of the Shaolin Queens of the Desert. If the fight I'm expecting does break out at the end of the competition, then the Post-Apocalypse Biker Girls are bound to take my side against Tank Girl and the Shaolin Queens. And, as the Wasteland Ninjas are already spoiling for a fight with the Shaolin Queens, I reckon the odds are now in our favour. There are the kangaroos to consider, of course, but they are very, very drunk. Tank, Sub and Jet Girls have their formidable weaponry, but it is all outside in the car park.

Yes, things have definitely taken a turn for the better. I wave to Iris Grim, leader of the Post-Apocalypse Biker Girls, and offer to buy her a drink. My hopes revive. If I end up being the winner, I reckon I now have a better than even chance of walking away safely with my winnings.

Unfortunately, these thoughts make me miss a chance to win a round, and it goes to Donner, another of the kangaroos. I curse. How is a man meant to play cards when Tank Girl is rambling on about Water and Power, and Ninjas and Shaolin Queens are fighting at the pool-table? Completely impossible. My pile of money continues to shrink. My hopes plummet.

In the bustle and confusion of the Post-Apocalypse Biker Girls' arrival, the fight between the Ninjas and the Shaolin Queens is smoothed over. The Biker Girls swarm towards the bar shouting for beer and crisps, shaking their head-dresses as they go, sending water flying around the room.

They bawl greetings to the Wasteland Ninjas and everyone else, apart from the Shaolin Queens, whom they ignore. Tank Girl, aware of their likely alliance against her, grunts in reply.

While all this is going on, I have decided that it is time for some direct action. I secrete the nine and ten of hearts up my sleeve. Next time it's my turn, and there is either a nine or a ten face-up on the table, I will whip out the appropriate card, which will, of course, enable me to shout '*snap!*' before anyone else knows what's happening. Shocking behaviour, of course. Quite unlike what you would expect from the popular and much-loved Trader, famed for his honesty from one end of the continent to the other, but necessary in the circumstances, I'm sure you will agree, faced as I am by the treacherous Tank Girl, one of the rawest cheats ever to blight the face of the earth.

7

'I foresee trouble,' says Sub Girl, which is the sort of thing that Sub Girl tends to say, in between long periods of gloomy silence. She has a reputation as something of a prophet, although it doesn't take much of a prophet to see that, if you put Tank Girl, the killer kangaroos, the Post-Apocalypse Biker Girls, the Wasteland Ninjas, the Shaolin Queens of the Desert and various other roughhouse miners, gangsters and freeloaders in a smoky bar-room for twenty-five hours and fill them full of beer, then there may well be trouble. Indeed, when, after a break in the game, Tank Girl comes back to find one of the Wasteland Ninjas occupying her seat, she pushes him off it in such a rough manner that it almost starts a fight there and then.

'Where was I?' she says, straddling her seat again.

'In the toilet,' answers Booga. Sadly, he is not making a joke.

'Deal the cards,' grunts Mining Jim, impatient to get going.

Tank Girl ignores him.

'I was talking about Kesslee.'

'And Sergeant Small,' puts in Jet Girl, her first words for some time. She seems to have her nausea under control and is making something of a comeback. How pleasant Jet Girl is. Why does such a nice young woman hang around with the truly appalling Tank Girl? I wonder if I might persuade her to give me a lift somewhere in her jet?

26

'Right,' says Tank Girl, lifting her beer. After twenty-five hours of enforced drinking no one else around the table is lifting their glass, except at the end of each game, when all the losers are obliged to drink, but Tank Girl drinks freely and continuously. I cannot deny that she has an amazing capacity for beer. Of course, an amazing capacity for beer is nothing to shout about. Doesn't make up for her numerous faults.

'Sergeant Small. Should I make a few jokes about his name and the size of his penis?'

'You usually do,' says Donner, whose appearance is fairly ludicrous even by kangaroo standards. He wears pink sun-glasses and a flowery waistcoat. Preposterous.

'Yes, I guess I do. Well, leaving the penis jokes aside for a moment, though I will come back to them, Sergeant Small was almost as big a creep as Kesslee. The first time I met ol' Jet Girl here, he was coming on to her in a truly repugnant fashion, and I was obliged to rescue her by snogging her, which seemed to put him off for a while. Jet Girl needed rescuing, of course, because she was just a shy little thing in those days, before I took her in hand and made her the woman she is today.'

'And a fine woman she is too,' says Donner.

I see that Donner is attached to Jet Girl. I feel jealous and wonder if I could come up with a good kebab joke.

Tank Girl drones on. She has taken off her jacket and is wearing a small ripped vest, which she quite deliberately lifts up in order to scratch her breasts. This is, of course, merely a cynical manoeuvre to break the concentration of Mining Jim. I am completely unaffected myself. It would take a good deal more than Tank Girl's breasts to put me off my cards.

'I was forced to work down in the repair pits, fixing the water pipes and making sandwiches, and a grim job it was too, dry, hot and difficult and the guards were utterly lacking in any sense of humour. Jet Girl was up in the hangars. Fixing jets, strangely enough.'

'Where was Sub Girl?'

'I hadn't met her yet. I expect she was away prophesying somewhere. Back then she spent most of her time making prophecies. Anyway, it was around then that I came up with the first of my brilliant escape plans, namely, rolling a stone in front of one of the automatic doors so it wouldn't shut properly, and sneaking out later.'

At this, the Professor sits up and speaks.

'You rolled a stone in front of one of the automatic doors so it wouldn't shut properly?'

'That's right.'

The Professor sniffs.

'I thought you said it was a huge, vast, technologically advanced military industrial complex?'

'It was.'

'Doesn't sound very advanced to me, if you could get out so easily. Not much of a security system, I mean.'

I chuckle. I can see that the Professor is as bored as I am with all this.

Tank Girl frowns, not pleased.

'It's all in the timing. I'm not saying just anyone could have made their escape like that. It took great skill and courage. And I had to find the right stone.'

'What was it like?'

'Never mind what the damn stone was like. Just take my word for it, it was right, and the whole affair took great skill and courage. And stop putting me off. I

28

escaped from my slave pen, avoided a few guards and got into a tank – a nice, friendly tank it seemed to me – but as soon as I got myself comfy and prepared to break my way out of the complex, the tank's computer started pissing around, demanding security codes and other really unreasonable stuff, which I was, naturally, unable to provide. Then the cockpit filled up with poisonous gas.'

Not poisonous enough, I reflect.

'So, things were looking fairly bleak at that moment, when Jet Girl arrived and switched off the gas. She understood things like security codes and computers. Lucky break for me, though I expect I would have escaped from the crisis somehow or other.'

Learning that Jet Girl saved Tank Girl's life, my esteem for her diminishes somewhat. Oh well, I suppose she was young at the time.

'So, that was that for that escape attempt. Whose deal is it?'

'Yours.'

Tank Girl deals out the cards and we start to play. And now even Tank Girl pays attention to the game. She leans wolf-like over the table, her braids and locks falling down over her eyes and her multiple earrings tinkling slightly as she follows the fall of cards round the table.

The Professor is next to me. I'm waiting for him to put down a nine or ten so I can whip out a hidden card from my sleeve and win the hand. He plays a three. It goes round again, each player playing the top card from their face-down bundle. No card of the same number falls twice. This time, the Professor's card is a seven. Damn him. All round again and no snap. The table is hushed. The watching crowd holds its breath. Well, not literally, I suppose. But they're slightly quieter than normal.

The rain beats down outside. By now it must be day thirty-seven of the rains. Three days to go. Why does it rain every year for forty days and forty nights? No one knows, not even the Professor. It does make everyone's life hell, though.

It's round to the Professor again. He plays a nine. With stunning dexterity and dazzling speed, I slip the nine out of my sleeve and slam it on to the pile.

'*Snap!*' I scream, before anyone else has time to react, and start scooping in the money.

I get some very suspicious looks from around the table. To hell with them. No one can prove a thing. I rake in the money gleefully, and everyone has to drink but me. Excellent. I can survive in the game for a while longer now and I notice that quite a few of the remaining players look very shaky indeed. I'll outdrink and outlast them all yet.

8

The atmosphere at the Annual Wastelands Snap and Drinking Competition has become noticeably strained. Rumours, and allegations of cheating and subterfuge are rife. Above the din I hear Big Mary complaining loudly to one of her barmen about the non-appearance of Alvin.

'That would have kept them in order for a while,' she grunts, and makes a few threats about what she'll do if Alvin does eventually show up.

I myself am rather disappointed at the non-appearance of Alvin, number-one rock star in the Wastelands. Not that I especially wanted to hear him play, my ears being a little too old to appreciate that sort of stuff these days, but I have some ancient artefacts with me that I'm sure he would be interested in. I've often sold him old music ephemera – books, records, a plectrum once used by Syd Barrett, that sort of thing – but now I have something of both great historical and practical value, namely a fuzzbox as used by the Sex Pistols in 1976. A working fuzzbox, the like of which you could not find today. The technology simply doesn't exist any more to make such an item. It's a miracle it survived beneath the desert sands for so long. Alvin is bound to pay me a load of money for it. After all, he claims to be a direct descendant of Donny Osmond, who, I know from my historical research, was a valued contemporary of the Sex Pistols.

As I was rather depending on Alvin buying the

fuzzbox to guarantee me having enough money to stay in the game, I hope he shows up. Also, it would calm things down if he played. Most of the gangs of people here like Alvin. Even Tank Girl, who doesn't really like anyone.

Mining Jim's friend Mining Pete, a vast mountain of a man in a blue tartan shirt, can't take another glass of beer. He tries to force it down, but it comes straight back up, and he slides slowly under the table. A few of the Shaolin Queens drag him away and dump him in a corner on top of some other comatose bodies, then sit down to watch the proceedings. Why do they wear their hair in topknots dyed red? I wonder. Almost as strange a hairstyle as that sported by Tank Girl, which is a mixture of shaved patches and coloured braids and dreadlocks. The Shaolin Queens' clothes glitter as the light above the table catches the mirror fragments sewn on to their black combat clothes. Muscles stand out on their forearms. They are tough women. I'm glad the Wasteland Ninjas and Post-Apocalypse Biker Girls outnumber them.

The Professor is dealing the next hand. Tank Girl is carrying on with her story. I still have the ten of hearts up my sleeve.

'So, after I failed to get away in the tank, I planned another escape. I used to talk about them in the showers with Jet here.'

Jet Girl shudders.

'The showers,' she says, making a face, 'they were gross.'

'Utterly gross,' agrees Tank Girl. 'Wasn't even water, just some chemical powder that scraped off the dirt. Disgusting. Diabolical. No good at all for the young lady of fashion.'

She whacks her fist down on the table.

'And just when I came up with this marvellous, majestic escape plan, it turned out they'd put a listening device in the showers. Perverts, I call them. Sergeant Small and a squadron or two of soldiers dragged me off to see Kesslee again, and he shot me full of poison darts.'

I find this part of the story a little hard to follow. Poison darts?

'Poison darts?'

'That's right, poison darts. You see, Kesslee was desperate to get me to work for him. "I must have Tank Girl working for me," he used to say. Understandable of course, anyone would want a woman like me on their side, but I kept refusing, so he tried to break my spirit by chaining me up in this little room and shooting poison darts into me. The darts had germs in them and gave me cholera and bubonic plague and yellow fever and a really bad attack of measles and, honestly, it was just a bad period in my life altogether. The only fun I had was when I heard that the Rippers, as they were called, had massacred some soldiers in the desert and destroyed some water-pipes. Which is the crux of the tale. Kesslee controlled the whole continent, apart from the Blue Dunes, and whenever soldiers went to the Blue Dunes they got massacred by these strange terrifying creatures called the Rippers. Kesslee wanted me to find them.'

'Why?' asks the Professor.

'What do you mean, why?'

'Why didn't he just send his huge, technologically advanced army to wipe them out? Or devastate the area with nuclear weapons? And why couldn't he find them with heat scanners or satellite imaging?'

Tank Girl frowns.

'Are you trying to spoil my story, Professor? I don't know why. He didn't invite me to his private councils. Maybe all the satellites were busy that week. All I know is, he was trying to get me to find them. I refused; he shot me full of diseases; I still refused; so he put me in this little narrow underground water-pipe. No room to move at all. Just me and the bubonic plague. Torture or what?'

The rain beats down. Tank Girl rambles on. Jet Girl wins the next hand and everyone forces down another beer. I start to feel terrible.

The door opens. Rain pours in. There is a general cheer in the bar. It's Alvin. With him are a bunch of young men in rancid denim, and yellow bandannas. I groan. It's the Post-Apocalypse Biker Boys with their dumb leader Marlin. Not unnaturally, they are deadly enemies of the Post-Apocalypse Biker Girls. In any ensuing fight they will side against them, and with Tank Girl. The odds have swung against me again.

I have had dealings with the Biker Boys. It was, in fact, me that inspired them, by selling them an ancient video of *The Wild One*. Watching it, Marlin was so impressed he named himself after Marlon Brando, the star. Unfortunately, he spelt it wrong and actually named himself after a fish. Standards of literacy are low these days in the Wastelands. The Biker Boys are particularly dumb.

Everyone is pleased to see Alvin.

'What kept you, you meat-head?' asks Big Mary, but even she likes him, and whacks a tankard into his hand. Alvin apologizes graciously for his late-coming, stating that his truck got stuck in a swamp some way down the road. As it has been raining for thirty-seven days, this is a reasonable excuse, although almost certainly not true. Alvin has most probably just woken up after some debauchery somewhere or other, but Big Mary lets it pass. Alvin is small and cute, and Big Mary has a soft spot for him. Most people have a soft spot for Alvin, the polite and cute little rock star, who looks like he has never shaved and will never need to, wears eye-liner behind his floppy fringe and sings songs about hopeless love.

It is well known that in his private life Alvin is completely debauched, spending his time ingesting huge cocktails of drugs while having sex with almost anything that moves, and would not know hopeless love if it came up and shook hands with him, but none the less, onstage he puts it across very well. During some of the quieter numbers people cry and think of better times.

The arrival of the Post-Apocalypse Biker Boys shakes my concentration, and I miss a chance to cheat with my ten. Tank Girl wins the hand, and the next two as well, and the pile of money in front of her is now the largest on the table. Unlike all the other players, her energy seems to increase as time wears on, and she becomes even louder and more obnoxious every time she wins.

'Another one to me,' she bawls, raking in her winnings and giving Booga a huge slap on the back that sends him crashing on to the table. 'Tank Girl triumphs again! Now where was I?'

'Just sitting at the table,' says Booga, quite seriously. I wonder, not for the first time, why Tank Girl chooses Booga the stupid kangaroo as a mate. I can find no reason for it. After all, Tank Girl, despite being a cheat, a liar and a thief, is thought very attractive by many people. Young men flock around her. Why choose a stupid, ugly kangaroo? Would a male hero go out with a female kangaroo? Very unlikely. Perhaps Tank Girl was the personal fantasy of the God who created her. Perhaps the God who created Tank Girl could not bear the thought of any man having her. Which does not say an awful lot for her creator.

Big Mary declares a break in the game, as she does occasionally. This gives the players the chance to visit the toilet, stretch their legs and try to get themselves back to something like human while Big Mary and her staff clear the table of glasses, ashtrays and bodies.

I am pleased at the break, as it gives me the chance to approach Alvin with a view to doing a little business. I lurch over to him very unsteadily and trip over a chair.

'Hello, Trader,' says Alvin, helping me to my feet.

'Got something for you. Sex Pistols' fuzzbox. Used by Steve Jones. Excellent item. Worth a load of money. Lain in the desert for years and years. Years and years and years. Worth plenty. Lain in the desert. For years. Years and years. Fuzzbox. Sex Pistols. Lain in the desert for years and years.'

I collapse again. Normally, as an experienced trader, I try to take a rather more polished approach to a sale, but with so much beer inside me my standards are slipping.

'Years and years and years,' I mutter, lying on top of Alvin's boots.

The band helps me into a chair. At the next table some Wasteland Ninjas are sniggering. Let them. They don't drink. Freaks.

'Years 'n' years,' I say, on the verge of passing out.

'Excuse me.'

36

I tumble off the chair and crawl towards the door. After some difficulty opening it, I plunge into the storm, sinking to my knees in the swamp outside. I'm sick. The rain is freezing. I feel a little better.

9

I am now wet through, which is most uncomfortable, but the coldness of the rain is refreshing. I stand around for a little while outside the Bar and Grill, but there is nothing really to look at, just floods everywhere and rain pouring down over the jet, the tank and the submarine which surround the Big Trader Truck. The Biker Gangs' machines are dotted around, and here and there are nondescript vans, including the ancient crimson ambulance that transports the Shaolin Queens of the Desert from one place to another. Hanging limply from the van is a flag, on which is painted some mystic symbol.

I'm not sure how Sub Girl got her submarine here. It's said that it can travel underground, but I don't believe it. Maybe she just floated here in the flood.

Well, that's enough about transportation in the Wastelands. I'm cold and wet, but I feel more able to cope with the prospect of another long session at cards. Tank Girl may be going strong at the moment, but she'll crack some time. I am also in a better state for a spot of trading, and I love trading.

Alvin is busy downing a few beers before heading onstage. I fetch my bag over and spill out the goodies on the table, all the valuable artefacts I've picked up here and there in the Wastelands: some found, some bought and some obtained by dubious means. There is the fuzzbox for Alvin and also some fairly valuable Carpenters videos, two yellowing *Doctor Who* comics, one platform shoe, a Lynyrd Skynyrd Greatest Hits album, unfortunately with a chunk missing out of it, a poster of Starsky and Hutch in excellent condition, a 'Vote for Jimmy Carter' campaign badge, a punctured orange Space Hopper and, rolled up in an advert for eight-track cartridge players, a genuine Donny Osmond cap. Alvin grabs the cap. I knew he'd like it.

'An interesting assortment, Trader.'

'Yep,' I grin. 'All the best, rarest 'seventies items, brought to you by the Trader after painstaking historical research and laborious archaeological digging. You won't find another Donny Osmond cap like that on the continent. And as for the fuzzbox . . .'

I point with pride to the back, where Steve Jones, the Sex Pistols' guitarist, has scratched his name.

'You see, it's fully authenticated.'

Alvin is impressed. Idiot. I scratched the name on the back myself. No one will ever know.

'What's that?' asks Gina, who plays in Alvin's band, pointing to the statue on the chair.

I shrug.

'Some statue of a woman. I found it in the desert. I thought the museum up in Lugit City might buy it.'

'It's got no arms,' she scoffs.

'I know. I suppose it isn't worth much. But they might pay me fifty zoobies.'

Lugit is the largest town on the continent, and I've sold a few other old things to the museum, mainly things that nobody else wanted.

Alvin is fingering the fuzzbox.

'Of course, it was made for a guitar,' I explain. 'And no one plays guitar any more, but just hook it up to one of your electronic boxes and it'll sound just fine.'

I have no idea if it will sound just fine or not, or whether it will even work, but it's worth a try. Alvin seems very keen, and I look forward to a big sale.

'Still got Syd Barrett's plectrum?'

He nods and shows me where he has attached it on the end of a chain that he wears around his neck as a lucky talisman. I grin, gather up my other goods and head back to the game. After the freezing rain and the bartering with Alvin, I feel better.

'Just made it,' mutters Mining Jim, as I clamber over a young Shaolin Queen of the Desert, who is sitting close to my position at the table.

'Ha ha, the Trader's been puking his guts up,' says Tank Girl. I maintain a dignified silence. The cards are dealt, and play continues. Tank Girl continues trying to put everyone off with her ridiculous story. Really, it's quite out of order, the way she keeps going on and on, quite cynically trying to break everyone's concentration. I would complain about her gross breach of the rules, except there aren't any rules in the Annual Wastelands Snap and Drinking Competition, apart from it being considered bad form to actually kill anyone before it's proved they were cheating.

'Well, after a while I got bored in the pipe, nothing to do there except lie around thinking "I'm in a pipe", which is not all that entertaining really, so I pretended I was desperate and called for help. Old Kesslee – have I described Kesslee? No? Well, he had sort of bleached white hair, a square jaw, and muscles, bit of a Nazi, really – that's enough to be going on with. Kesslee thought I was giving up, but when they dragged me back into the office I just abused him as per usual and boy, was he mad! Totally furious. He ranted and raved when I told him it took more than a few days in a pipe with bubonic plague to break my spirit. The iron will of Tank Girl just refused to crack, and it really burned his ass. Because it wasn't just that he thought I could help find the Rippers, who kept massacring his soldiers – he had this thing about wanting to break my will.'

'No one can break your will, Tank Girl,' says Booga, who is a truly disgusting sycophant.

'Not like I broke yours,' replies Tank Girl, and screams with laughter, although if there is a joke in there it escapes me. She scratches her breasts again, and Mining Jim completely fails to notice that he should have won the hand.

'Anyway, I got hauled out and driven with a lot of soldiers in a convoy to some especially God-forsaken part of the desert and shoved into this funny little elevator that went down into the sand. Called a subgate, I think. They wanted me to find out if the Rippers lived there.'

'Why, with all their technology, did they not just send down a robot probe?' enquires the Professor. 'Much easier, surely?'

Tank Girl looks cross again.

'How the hell would I know? I wasn't responsible for the actions of these people.'

'*Snap!*' says the Professor, having successfully diverted everyone's attention from the game. He is a wily old man, the Professor. Tank Girl is furious.

'How can a girl play cards when you're talking all the time?' she demands. 'What are you doing here anyway? Shouldn't you be away studying a book or something?'

'*Doctum pecunia ipsum iuvat,*' replies the Professor. 'Money is pleasing even to a scholar.'

41

'Well, stop interrupting my story: we're just reaching an exciting bit.'

It's been a long time coming. I notice that Mining Pete is looking very shaky in his seat. Wanda, foremost gun dealer on the continent, does not look at all well either. Wanda has a large pile of money in front of her. She's a good card-player and a fair drinker but I think she's going to crack soon.

'Just as they were going to put me in the subgate, the Rippers attacked. Huge monstrous beasts tearing and slashing everywhere. Water and Power soldiers were cut to shreds, limbs flew in all directions, it was carnage all round. Really, it was the only fun I'd had in ages. There were a few blows aimed in my direction but, of course, it takes more than a savage Ripper to get me, what with me learning to ride a buffalo when I was three and surviving on my own in the desert since I was four, so I just stepped out the way and watched what was going on. Good battle, though, one of the best.

'After this the Rippers departed, leaving a lot of dead soldiers, and me. And Kesslee's forearm, I seem to remember, which had been cut off in the battle. Kesslee escaped, though. I took out a knife and cut out the tracking probe Kesslee had inserted in my arm – or was it my leg? I can't remember. He'd stuck a probe somewhere on my body, but I probably wasn't paying much attention at the time. Anyway, I got rid of it and wondered what to do with the rest of my life. Armed insurrection against Kesslee? Prolonged guerilla warfare against the state? Open a restaurant? Skiing holiday? The possibilities seemed endless, but then Jet Girl arrived, looking pleased with herself. I gave her a friendly greeting.

' "Hello, Jet Girl, you dumb hippy deadbrain, what are you looking so pleased about?" ' She'd finally got herself together, given Sergeant Small the brush-off, and a knee to the groin, stolen a jet fighter and left Water and Power headquarters. She landed beside me, and it was at this point that I acquired my now famous tank, as may be seen parked outside next to the submarine. And a faithful friend that tank has proved to me over the past years, I must say. Yes sir, that tank and me are inseparable. I love it. It loves me. We drink together, sleep together, have adventures together, watch TV, shower, go to the shops, do everything together. Honestly, I'd be lost without it. No young woman of any standing should be without one.'

'I love my submarine,' says Sub Girl. 'I built it with my own hands.'

Rather unlikely story this, it seems to me. Surely it takes more than one person to build a large submarine? Never mind, Tank Girl is still rambling on, while I endeavour to keep track of the cards as they're played.

'So, me and Jet just decided to hang out in the desert together and have fun. Which we did. But after a while –'

The Professor plays a ten. I still have a ten secreted up my sleeve. I whip it out unobserved and play it, calling *snap!* immediately.

I start shovelling in the money, but Tank Girl interrupts me.

'Why is that card wet?' she demands.

I see with horror that the card *is* wet. It is, in fact, completely soggy, having been up my sleeve when I left the bar to go outside into the rain.

There is an awkward pause.

'Because it's lying in a puddle of beer,' I say, with a hurt tone in my voice, as if anyone could be casting aspersions on my honesty.

There is a lot of beer on the table.

Tank Girl leans over the table, positioning her face a few inches from mine.

'I'd hate to think that you were cheating, Trader.'

An angry Tank Girl is a frightening sight. I assume the nonchalant air I generally use when buying valuable heirlooms cheaply off the elderly and infirm.

'What's the matter, Tank Girl? Can't take another glass of beer?'

Tank Girl is taken aback. Almost the worst thing that anyone could think about her is that she can't take another glass of beer. She is so annoyed at this slur on her name that she immediately sits down and drinks her beer to prove me wrong, and after this everyone else drinks. Well, by tradition all arguments about any round in this game are assumed to have ended when everyone has drunk, so the matter now has to be forgotten.

Tank Girl is exceedingly displeased but makes no further comment. I have for the meantime outsmarted her, which is not all that hard. She may be fierce but she's not the cleverest woman ever to walk the planet.

With the rain pounding on the windows, Tank Girl and Jet Girl get to reminiscing about the old days in the desert, when there wasn't any water.

'Couldn't take a shower.'

'Or have a bath.'

'Or clean your teeth.'

'Or wash your clothes.'

'Or wash your hair.'

'Or play with toy boats.'

'Or go for a swim.'

'Or throw bread for the ducks.'

'Or skim flat stones over a pool.'

'Or throw people in a river fully clothed on a cold night.'

'Or splash about in puddles.'

'Or run the tank through puddles so everyone around got wet.'

'Or water-ski.'

'Or aqualung.'

'Or dive.'

'Or surf.'

'There must have been a sea somewhere you could surf in,' says the Professor.

'Suppose so,' agrees Tank Girl, 'but we could never find it. Anyway, the sea is no good for cleaning your teeth. Too salty and the seaweed sticks to your fillings. But the suffering caused by all the above was as nothing compared to the perpetual beer crisis. You might find it hard to believe, but there were actually days when we couldn't get any beer at all.'

She stops, shuddering at the horror of the memory.

'Can you imagine? No beer! All wells and other sources of water were under the control of Water and Power and, naturally, they didn't use the water to make beer for the general public. They kept it all to themselves. The soldiers used to walk around deliberately swigging cans of lager while the suffering public was forced to look on in torment.

'There were a few small, illegal breweries hidden in valleys where people had found their own wells and used the water to make their own brew, but it was a dangerous business. Hunting down these illegal breweries was a number-one priority for Water and Power. Even if they survived undetected, it didn't necessarily mean that Jet and me could get beer from them. There was so little of it around that sometimes they wouldn't even sell a pint to a desperate woman, claiming they needed it all themselves. Such staggering meanness, it used to drive me insane. Had it been me with my own brewery, I would have distributed the product freely. Tank Girl is famed for her generosity.'

She is not. Famed for her stupidity, maybe.

'"Jet Girl," I used to say, "we have to do something about this. Prolonged abstinence from beer is having a ruinous effect on my health and spoiling my sunny disposition. What we need is our own brewery. Let's think of a plan."

'We thought for a while.

'"What we need first," I said, "is our own source of water."'

'Didn't I say that?' asks Jet Girl.

'No, it was me. You said we should design the beer cans first. So we hunted around in the desert for water for a while, but it was pretty hopeless. I mean, have you ever tried finding a hidden underground stream in a hurry? Just doesn't happen. Then, I remembered there used to be people called water-diviners, who wandered around holding a couple of sticks, and the sticks started to shake, or point, or something whenever they walked over a hidden source of water but, when we tried to find a water-diviner, we were unsuccessful. They'd all been put in prison by Kesslee. He'd declared that all water-diviners were dangerous subversives.

'By now I was completely frustrated. Water and Power had closed down all the illegal breweries we knew of and there was just no beer to be had anywhere.

'"To hell with this," I said. 'I'll find some water myself. There can't be too much to it. All you have to do is walk around waving a couple of sticks. I can do that."

'So, I sent Jet Girl off in her jet to find some hops and some barley and a recipe book for making beer while I got busy with the sticks.'

Tank Girl purses her lips.

'Have you ever tried walking over a burning-hot desert waving a couple of sticks? Completely stupid enterprise. Felt like a fool. Eventually, I figured out that it might be easier if I just sat on the back of my tank and trundled along, so I tried this for a while, sitting on my deck-chair holding the sticks, waiting for them to start shaking, or twitching, or whatever. I always enjoy sitting on the back of my tank: it's very comfortable up there. As well as the deck-chair, I've got a fridge, a table, an armchair, a barbecue, some of my favourite bric-a-brac and, of course, the world-famous collection of Tank Girl weaponry – guns, missiles, baseball bats and catapults from all corners of the earth. All in excellent taste, of course. Only last month a man came down from the art gallery in Lugit City, wanting to put it in an exhibition. "Installations from Duchamp to Tank Girl". Duchamp, of course, was well known for decorating tanks.

'Anyway, we'd been driving along for a couple of hours or so, and I was becoming more and more discouraged, when, suddenly, the sticks started shaking and vibrating like mad. The signal was so powerful that the whole tank shook! Wow! I thought. This is incredible. Must be an underground river at least. And you know what it was?'

'You'd found a well?' asks Booga.

'No,' says Tank Girl. 'I'd crashed into a government beer truck. Killed the driver instantly, and spilled crates everywhere. Huge truck it was; there were cans of beer rolling about in all directions. So, when Jet .arrived back, we just gathered it all up and made off to our hide-out for a good drink. Of course, afterwards Jet Girl put the whole incident down to blind luck, but it wasn't. It was sheer talent on my part. Other water-diviners can only find little streams and stuff like that. I located a whole beer truck.'

'Tank Girl, you are fabulous,' says Booga.

'Thank you,' says Tank Girl.

'*Puella Testudo mendax sus est*,' murmurs the Professor.

'What's that?' asks Tank Girl.

'Nothing, nothing,' says the Professor mildly, which

is just as well, as, when I ask him later, he informs me it is Latin for 'Tank Girl is a lying swine'.

Before the next hand gets under way my attention is diverted by a tug on my sleeve.

It is Magdalen, leader of the Shaolin Queens of the Desert. As well as a bright red column of hair sticking up on her head, she has four rings in her nose and thirty-two in her ears – a Wastelands record, I believe.

'How much are you selling the statue for?' she asks.

'The statue? Well . . .'

I'm about to say that it is not really worth all that much, but, of course, my natural trader's instinct takes over.

'Well, the museum up in Lugit City is always frantic to get hold of old statues. I figure they'll pay me 1000 zoobies for it.'

Magdalen snorts, which is quite difficult to do when you're whispering.

'You're lying. The museum doesn't have that sort of money these days. They'll pay you ten if you're lucky. The Shaolin Queens will offer you twenty-five zoobies for it.'

'I can't go under 900.'

'Thirty. Take it or leave it. But, if you leave it, we will be obliged to offer definite proof to Tank Girl that you cheated in the last round. Four of us saw you bring that ten of hearts out of your sleeve.'

'Ehm, let me think about this one, Magdalen,' I say, slightly distressed.

The next hand starts and Jet Girl wins it and the next one quickly. I'm trying to think what to do for the best, and it's difficult, what with having to drink beer all the time and Magdalen threatening me and Tank Girl still casting very suspicious glances in my direction. I've no idea why the Shaolin Queens would want the statue, but I don't want to let it go for thirty zoobies. The museum will pay me fifty, I'm sure. There's so little culture around these days that they're always keen to get another relic, even a dull one like the one I'm selling.

Magdalen's threat is quite worrying, though. Really, it is strange how the simple business of trading can get you into terrible difficulties. Only last month John the Brute, Bandit King of the Red Mountains, curse his name, threatened to tear me to pieces with his bare hands after imagining, quite incorrectly, that I'd swindled him in an arms deal.

Really, I was entirely innocent and was merely acting as a go-between for Wanda the Gun Dealer. The accusation that I had pocketed a substantial portion of the profits for myself was never substantiated, and Wanda believed me.

I understand John the Brute is still annoyed about it. I haven't been back to the Red Mountains to check it out.

Still, I digress. I don't like Magdalen threatening me in this way and I don't see why I should make twenty zoobies less on the statue than I was expecting, what with money being so hard to come by these days. But my mind is made up for me when, after a run of extremely bad luck in the game, I find myself without enough to stake myself in for the next hand.

I seek out Magdalen and make the sale. She hands over the thirty zoobies, which lets me continue in the game. Not too bad for an old statue, really, I think, making the best of it. The museum might not have wanted it anyway. So, the Shaolin Queens of the Desert now own the statue, and good luck to them. Magdalen mentions they have been looking for a new representation of the Goddess for a while, although I don't care if they use it as a Goddess or a hat-stand.

'Are you going to take it away just now?' I ask.

'No. We have to stay around till the end of the game to pick up our bets from ZugZug the Bookmaker. We'll leave it where it is till it's time to go.'

I glance over at the statue. One of the Shaolin Queens has draped her combat jacket over its shoulders. On the chair in the dark corner, it looks quite lifelike.

I lose again. Every time I call *snap!* I am much too late, and someone else is raking in the zoobies. My concentration is way off. The pile of money in front of me starts to shrink again. Everything seems to be difficult these days. I'm more or less cursing my luck and wondering why things refuse to get better, when the door opens with an extremely loud crash and a group of large, mean-faced individuals walk in, followed by some small, even meaner-faced individuals, followed by John the Brute, Bandit King of the Red Mountains, last seen threatening to tear me apart with his bare hands.

'Okay!' bawls Tank Girl. 'I got a gutful of beer, a handful of cards and a nose full of snot; it's day thirty-eight of the rainy season; and it's now time to clean up you suckers, so let's play!'

She whacks down the first card of the next round and off we go again. With so much beer inside her, Tank Girl is becoming even more manic and starts balancing on the back of her chair, simultaneously playing snap and telling her story.

'So there I was, free at last, with a tank of my own, in the desert.'

She starts miming driving the tank, which seems to involve lots of grinding of gears and jamming down of the accelerator and going 'Boom! Boom!' as she fires the gun. Meanwhile, Jet Girl is getting into the spirit of things and explaining that she was flying around up above in her jet, at which both she and Tank Girl hold out their arms like wings and go 'Whee! Whee!' The kangaroos laugh and Tank Girl pretends to be shooting at them with her tank and starts tossing peanuts around the table so that the more sober onlookers, such as myself, Mining Jim and the Professor, have to continually dodge the barrage of missiles whilst endeavouring to maintain some level of concentration. Eventually, Mining Jim protests and Tank Girl roars with laughter and sticks out her tongue at him. Really, it's a miracle no one's killed her yet.

I, meanwhile, am slouched in my seat, partly to avoid

the flying peanuts and partly in the vain hope that John the Brute, Bandit King of the Red Mountains, and his evil-smelling and extremely violent entourage don't notice me.

Were it not for the fact that John the Brute has recently taken such an unfortunate dislike to me, I might actually have welcomed his arrival. Not on personal grounds, as John the Brute is the last person you'd want to invite to any sort of social gathering, but because of his well-known hatred of Tank Girl. The presence of him and his companions certainly swings the balance of odds against her.

Despite the fact that, as far as I know, they have never actually met, the animosity between Tank Girl and John the Brute is intense, going back to certain incidents last year, in which several large beer convoys heading for the Red Mountains were mysteriously hijacked by three female figures wearing Kermit the Frog masks and wielding baseball bats. Tank Girl blithely denied all knowledge of the events when confronted by ambassadors sent down from the Red Mountains to find out what was happening to their beer supplies but, as she, Jet Girl and Sub Girl were actually found floating contentedly in a large swimming-pool filled entirely with imported lager, her denials were hard to believe. Since then threats and insults have flown back and forth between the Wastelands and the Red Mountains. Now that Tank Girl and John the Brute are together in the same room, something bad is bound to happen. John the Brute is not the sort of man to let the hijacking of his beer convoys go unavenged.

It is very unusual for the Bandit King to leave the Red Mountains and risk running into government soldiers. The government is a bit of a joke these days, of course, but, occasionally, a patrol will come down from Lugit City and nose around for a while. So he must have a powerful reason for making the journey into the Wastelands, and his arrival has caused great surprise and shock to everybody in the Bar and Grill. Apart from Tank Girl. Despite everything, she is pretending not to notice.

'Yes sir, it was fun in the desert in those days,' she continues. 'Just riding round in the old tank, playing with buffalos and having the odd skirmish with Water and Power soldiers. They were always coming around, demanding their tank back, and I had to keep blasting them out of existence: this was fine most of the time, before it became a little boring. That was when I had the extra-brilliant idea of disguising the tank.'

'It was my idea,' says Jet Girl, shaking her long black hair.

'Whatever,' says Tank Girl. 'We went to this workshop in the middle of nowhere to get a couple of paint jobs for the tank and the jet and who do you think we met there? Noddy and Big Ears! No, I'm lying, it was Sub Girl. She didn't have a submarine in those days, of course, but you could see it was only a matter of time. She was obviously a submarine type of girl. I mean, she used to go around saying stuff like "the rains are coming, the rains are coming". In fact, now I think about it, that's all she ever did say, which made for some odd conversations if, for instance, you were just asking her if she'd like a cup of tea.'

'It never rained in those days,' says Sub Girl, who, with her funny part-shaved hairstyle and strangely mismatched leather clothes, looks not unlike Tank Girl. 'It hadn't rained since the comet. But I could see rain in the future.'

As it now rains every year for forty days and forty nights without a break, it's hard to argue with this one.

'We did the most fabulous paint jobs on the tank and the jet. My tank just loved it. It was all washes of bright colours and chrome and cadillac stickers, a rolling funking war-machine fit for a girl of my standing in the community. And we would probably have gone on, just wandering around the desert having a good time, if Sub Girl hadn't let slip that Little Wee Sam was a prisoner at the Liquid Silver Good Time Bordello. Which was bad news, if you remember that Little Wee Sam was only ten at the time the soldiers kidnapped her from the hippy commune and completely innocent of the wicked ways of the world.'

Little Wee Sam continues to snore drunkenly under the table, though her hand seems to have made its way between her legs. I expect Tank Girl has been a bad influence on her.

'So, what did we do?'

'Tell us, Tank Girl,' asks Booga enthusiastically, ears flopping about in a particularly stupid manner.

'We set out to rescue her!'

The kangaroos cheer.

'*Snap!*' screams Tank Girl, winning the hand. I drink, and grimace. It's Mining Jim's deal. He shuffles the cards.

Tank Girl seems to have lost the plot somewhat and is now going on about Kesslee and his robot-arm.

'He had this cyber-arm full of weapons and buzz-saws and stuff sewn on in place of the one he'd lost in the fight with the Rippers. He let out afterwards that he'd had the surgery done with no anaesthetic because he was immune to pain, but I expect he was lying. Mind you, he was a strange kind of guy. Practically no sense of humour at all. One time, when I was his prisoner, I put a dog turd on his favourite chair just before he sat on it and he absolutely refused to see the funny side. Had four of his guards executed, I remember. Anyway, enough of silly old Kesslee for now, although it is important to remember that he and his evil henchmen were still ruling the world at the time I'm talking about, and causing misery everywhere with excessive taxes and general tyranny.'

Bored with Tank Girl's tedious ramblings, I let my eyes wander to the far side of the room. Through the smoke I notice that John the Brute is glaring over at us, but whether he is directing his evil stare at me or at Tank Girl, I'm not sure. At her, I hope.

. She burps, and drinks down another beer, as does Sub Girl. I'm slightly suspicious of Sub Girl. She's been going along quietly, winning a few hands, drinking her beer without showing too many ill effects, conserving her energy. It wouldn't surprise me if she's in the contest right to the end.

While Mining Jim is shuffling the cards, the Professor leans over to me, a learned glint in his eye. I am a little worried by this, as it is not unknown for the Professor to quote lines of Latin. I always find this a little disturbing because, as far as I know, he is the only person in the entire world still able to understand Latin, and I'm always stuck for an answer. On this occasion, however, he spares me the ancient quotes, but does come up with something very interesting.

'I greatly appreciated the books you found for me,

Trader. *The Vicar of Wakefield* was particularly fine. So I have some advice for you. Don't sell that statue to the Shaolin Queens for thirty zoobies. Or to the museum for fifty.'

'Why not?'

'Because it is the *Venus de Milo*.'

'The what?'

'The *Venus de Milo*. Haven't you heard of it?'

I shake my head. The 'seventies is my period, you understand.

'It was one of the most famous works of art in the world in the old days, before the comet struck. It's fantastically valuable. Completely priceless. Even on this God-forsaken continent it must be worth about 1,000,000 zoobies.'

I'm dumbstruck – 1,000,000 zoobies?

'You're joking.'

'I'm entirely serious.'

'But it can't be worth that much,' I protest, 'it doesn't have any arms. They must have got broken off when the comet struck.'

The Professor says it never had any arms, even before the comet. Apparently it doesn't matter. It's still priceless.

I'm appalled. I've just sold 1,000,000 zoobies' worth of statue to the Shaolin Queens for a measly thirty. Why couldn't the Professor tell me earlier?

'1,000,000 zoobies,' I groan.

'Did somebody just say "1,000,000 zoobies"?' asks Tank Girl, leaning over the table, ears flapping. I clam up immediately.

12

Big Mary is hovering in the background with a mop
and bucket, and I see that she is just waiting for this
hand to finish before she announces the next break in
play. I also see that, in addition to the two revolvers in
her apron, she is now carrying a small shotgun strapped
over her back, and I imagine she is slightly concerned
about the arrival of John the Brute in her Bar and Grill.
John the Brute generally just roams around the Red
Mountains robbing anyone who comes his way. He is
not known for his social calls. His arrival can only
mean trouble.

As well as his usual entourage of thuggish body-
guards, including Loretta Dragon Slayer, Kung Fu
champion of the continent, he is protected by the Four
Dwarfs, and the Four Dwarfs are utterly grim. I mean,
they're not friendly little dwarfs with red hats and
cheery faces: they're horrible, mean, violent dwarfs
about four feet tall and five feet wide with muscles like
beer barrels and fists like sledgehammers, and they each
carry a massive axe slung over their shoulders. They are
just not the sort of people you'd want to sit down to
dinner with. Particularly if their boss is of the opinion
that you have swindled him in an arms deal.

Well, with all this going on and the information from the
Professor regarding the value of the statue, I find it hard to
concentrate on the game, and I miss a chance to win the
next hand, which is taken by Sub Girl. We all drink. I feel
nauseous. Big Mary bustles up to announce a break.

I slip away from the table, but I am immediately grabbed by Loretta Dragon Slayer, who is flanked by two of the dwarfs, with axes.

'John the Brute wants to talk to you,' she says.

'I'm busy at the moment,' I reply. 'Would two o'clock tomorrow be convenient?'

Loretta takes my arm in a nerve-numbing death-grip and marches me across the room. Okay, I'll go and talk to John the Brute.

The Wasteland Ninjas, Post-Apocalypse Biker Girls, Post-Apocalypse Biker Boys and the Shaolin Queens of the Desert are all sprawled around the bar drinking heavily, but they look on with interest as Loretta Dragon Slayer, clad in a fairly becoming silver Samurai outfit, escorts me over to the corner. John the Brute is waiting for me, although I fail to detect any signs of welcoming pleasure in his heavily scarred face as I arrive. I decide to brazen it out.

'Hello, John the Brute, Bandit King of the Red Mountains,' I say, fairly cheerily. 'How nice to see you away from your usual haunts. I was just saying the other day, how pleasant it would be if you were to stop hiding yourself away in the Red Mountains and visit us down here in the Wastelands. We've all missed you. How is everything? Still plenty of people to rob I trust?'

John the Brute, eight feet tall at least, picks me up and thrusts his face close to mine.

'I ought to kill you here on the spot,' he snarls. Behind him, the dwarfs chuckle.

'Kill me? Me? The honest and popular Trader? Surely you're confusing me with someone else?'

He squeezes me so hard it is difficult to breathe.

'You swindled me in the arms deal.'

'Not at all,' I gasp.

'Yes, you did. Money went missing somewhere between me and Wanda the Gun Dealer.'

'It's the postal service again,' I suggest. 'It's terrible these days.'

John the Brute gives me a light tap on the head. I am knocked practically unconscious.

'You took it. Don't bother denying it. But I didn't come here for that. John the Brute does not travel long distances merely to retrieve a little money from a Wasteland worm like yourself. I'm here for the statue.'

Again, I find this a little hard to follow.

'Pardon?'

'The statue. The *Venus de Milo*. I know you have it, because it was in the back of your truck when you went to O'Halleran's garage after you left the Red Mountains. O'Halleran is a friend of mine.'

I curse. What a mistake to show it there. Of course, I didn't know what it was then. And who would have expected O'Halleran to be able to identify a valuable work of art? After a few drinks he couldn't identify his own mother. Well, in truth, nobody could identify O'Halleran's mother, but you know what I mean.

'Kindly put me down so we can discuss the matter fully.'

He drops me, and I thump on to the floor. The dwarfs chuckle. Beer churns around inside me, and I try urgently to order my thoughts.

'Eh, why do you want it?' I enquire politely, trying to gain a little time.

'A present for my partner,' he says. 'Juliet, Bandit Queen of the Red Mountains.'

The dwarfs do not chuckle. He must be serious.

At the far end of the room Alvin and his band are tuning up, and Tank Girl is screaming her head off about something or other.

'Well, John the Brute, I will be delighted to do business with you, and look forward to opening negotiations on the matter at the earliest opportunity. But, I have to tell you, you are not the only buyer in the market. Already, I have received several generous bids, and interest is growing all the time. It is not every day that the world's foremost art treasure turns up on the open market.'

John the Brute narrows his eyes and looks very mean indeed.

'Has Tank Girl made a bid?' he asks suspiciously. 'If she's after it, I'll kill her.'

'She has expressed a vague interest,' I lie, trying desperately to keep all my options open.

'I'll give you 200 zoobies,' says John.

'Well, I don't think that you can expect to pick up such an item at a knock-down price like that,' I say. 'Not a good enough offer to make me remove it from the extremely secure, hidden, well-guarded vault in which it now resides.'

This is a fairly desperate bluff on my part, as the *Venus de Milo*, far from being in a well-guarded vault, is, at this moment, actually sitting round the card-table. Still, it's very gloomy in here, and she is wearing a baseball cap and a black combat jacket, so there is a chance he won't notice.

John the Brute grunts.

'How about if I just rip you to shreds, as promised?'

'Then the excellent Juliet, Bandit Queen of the Red

Mountains, would never get the *Venus de Milo* to decorate her boudoir,' I reply.

He looks thoughtful, and I take the opportunity to scurry back to the table, all the while thinking frantically. I could have just told the Bandit King that I'd already sold the statue to the Shaolin Queens, but I've no intention of letting this priceless item disappear for only thirty zoobies. Somehow, I will have to wangle it back from Magdalen.

13

'Liquid Silver!' says Tank Girl, as the game resumes. 'Used to be the pleasure centre of the world. Cheap postcards of the desert and a five-star buffalo-burger restaurant. Late-night drinking and gambling, and no scum like me allowed in. And the Liquid Silver Good Time Bordello, where men who had the money would come to be entertained by singers, dancers, strippers and prostitutes. Water and Power owned it, like they owned everything.

'Now, Sam had been sent here after being captured, and it was definitely my duty to rescue her.'

'And we had nothing better to do that weekend,' puts in Jet Girl.

'And we had nothing better to do that weekend,' agrees Tank Girl. 'So we drove there in the tank and politely asked the guard to let us in. "Okay, pizza-face," I said to him, "move your ass before you get hurt."

'He didn't move, so I slugged him. I never like wasting a lot of time with doormen. When I got inside, some unpleasant woman came up to me, and I was going to slug her as well, but then I realized she thought I was there looking for work.'

She throws back her head and laughs.

'Can you imagine me working as a prostitute?'

'Yes,' murmurs the Professor, and Mining Jim and Wanda the Gun Dealer and me, but we mutter it quietly.

'So I followed her up to the preparation room, which was a kind of booth, where a computer told you what to do to become the perfect prostitute, that is, put on a long slinky dress and high heels and nice make-up and stuff, which, naturally, I declined to do, as long slinky dresses just don't suit me at all and high heels are terrible for your spine. But they did have a fairly groovy little machine for putting in earrings, which I used to punch rings into my ears and a few other places, and I screwed around with the hairdressing machine so it gave me a few extensions on my locks and dyed bits and pieces of my hair green and yellow. All in all, with the dyed locks and blood still dripping out of where I'd pierced myself, and my ever trusty motorbike boots, I have to admit I was looking pretty good. Eyecatching even.

'When I left the booth, I was immediately in trouble. There were these guards everywhere, and the first one that saw me realized right away that something had gone wrong. I don't know why, possibly it was the way I'd put lipstick under my eyes. He started shouting at me, so I used the earring machine to punch a few earrings through his cheeks, and after that he just lay around moaning, and I went off to look for Sam.

'The bordello was tacky, extra tacky, all marble floors and jacuzzis and suchlike, set at weird angles and kind of running into each other. Reminded me of a Salvador Dali poster they used to have in the hippy commune, but worse. Upstairs were private rooms. I started to search them, which was quite an interesting experience, what with various perversions going on in them. Some of them were really quite intriguing and made me think a bit about how it was time to improve my sex life, providing I could ever find a suitable partner. I can't honestly say that the people in the rooms I entered were thrilled to see me – usually they tried to hide under the bedclothes or threw pillows at me – and soon there was quite a fuss, with clients running everywhere, demanding their money back. Fortunately, at this moment I heard Sam's voice crying out from the next room.

'She was shouting, "Don't touch me, you bad man, I am only ten years old and completely innocent!" or something like that, anyway. So, I burst in to rescue her but, when I got there, she was doing not badly herself. She had a danger-ball, one of Water and Power's fantastically advanced weapons, which explodes, then re-forms itself so you can use it again.'

'Scientifically impossible,' says the Professor.

'None the less, she had one,' says Tank Girl, pointedly. 'And she'd used it to explode the man's hand off. It was no more than he deserved, as I explained to him as he was lying there bleeding.

'"That's what you get for being an old perv, pissface," I told him, quite sternly, and we departed. Sam was thrilled beyond measure to see me, of course, and wept tears of joy as we raced downstairs. By now there were guards running everywhere, but I single-handedly fought them off with my trusty baseball bat –'

'No, you didn't,' says Jet Girl. 'I sneaked in the back way and helped you.'

'Jet Girl helped a little,' concedes Tank Girl. 'But it was me that put a gun to the chief Madam's head and threatened to blow it off if they didn't all put down their guns and let us go. A trick I learned from various episodes of *Kojak* I've seen over the years. We went outside, leapt into the tank, picked up a few buffalo-burgers and a cup of tea and drove off, singing songs. That was that, really. Sam rescued, nice new outfit and haircut for me, and back to the desert for some fun and relaxation. Liquid Silver was in chaos, I'm pleased to say. I always like to leave chaos behind me. Doesn't feel quite right otherwise.

'I got busy fitting up some deck-chairs and garden furniture on top of my tank so I could get a real good tan in between bouts of mayhem, destruction and drinking. Which reminds me . . .'

She finishes her beer and calls loudly for more.

'You don't have the balls to outdrink me, Trader,' she sneers. 'None of you do.' She pours down another.

The next part of Tank Girl's tale is insufferably tedious, consisting of endless stories of drinking and sunbathing with her tank. She talks about her tank as if it was a friend, which demonstrates what a strange person she is, or maybe that she's just short of friends. While she is going on, however, I do notice her casting a few glances in the direction of John the Brute, and I can see that, although she has not deigned to acknowledge his presence, she is well aware that there is almost certainly trouble in store. Some of the messages Tank Girl sent to John the Brute after the business with the beer convoys were of such an insulting nature that it will be almost impossible for him to let them pass unanswered. Whatever the outcome of this, their first encounter, I can't imagine it will be peaceful.

If John the Brute's story is true, about wanting the statue for Juliet, then he did not come to Big Mary's Bar and Grill specifically to meet Tank Girl, but he must have known it was likely she would be here. Tank Girl always plays in the Annual Wastelands Snap and

Drinking Competition. I can only suppose that this is why he is accompanied not only by his usual thugs but also the Four Dwarfs and Loretta Dragon Slayer. Loretta has a truly awesome reputation as a fighter. Well, I mean, anyone who goes around slaying dragons must know how to look after themselves. And you don't see many dragons around these days, so she must be good at it.

If things turn nasty we are in for quite a battle, and I wonder how I can come out on top, or at least come out of it alive.

I glance round at all the various forces arrayed in the bar-room and weigh up the odds, as I see them. Most probably it would be John the Brute, Loretta Dragon Slayer, the Four Dwarfs, the Wasteland Ninjas and the Post-Apocalypse Biker Girls versus Tank Girl, Jet Girl, Sub Girl, the kangaroos, the Shaolin Queens and the Post-Apocalypse Biker Boys. Quite a battle indeed. I'm not sure who would win. Of course, Tank Girl has never lost a fight. There again, neither has John the Brute.

The card-game continues, now made more difficult, as Alvin has started to play on the small stage at the end of the room. The noise is deafening, and anyone calling *snap!* has to scream at the top of their voice. Keeping concentration in these circumstances is extremely difficult, and only my grim determination to win money keeps me going. The only advantage is that the noise temporarily forces Tank Girl to stop telling her story, or at least it stops me from hearing it. The last thing she says is something like, 'But then that idiot Sam went and got herself kidnapped again by Water and Power, and they took her to their headquarters,' before the din makes further talk impossible. I'm not clear about how Sam got kidnapped again. I don't care. I don't expect Tank Girl cared either, unless it was Sam's turn to buy the drinks.

14

I notice that Ootsie, young apprentice of the Wasteland Ninjas, has left his fellow Ninjas playing pool and worked his way through the bar-room crowd. He is now standing directly behind Sub Girl, looking on. Sub Girl pays no attention to him, as her concentration on the game is intense, even in the midst of all this clamour.

The Undersea Queen of the Deep is a woman of few words and does not join in either with Tank Girl's banter or the raucous singing along with Alvin that is now taking place in the bar-room. Even Mining Jim, a large middle-aged man in a grubby vest, who is not given to pop music of any variety, is tapping his foot under the table, his inhibitions weakened by the twenty-seven-hour drinking bout. Sub Girl sits motionless, however, eyes fixed on the play, concentration intact.

Ever since Ootsie entered the bar, I've noticed he seems to be distracted by the women here. Understandable, I suppose. There are no women in the Wasteland Ninjas. Almost all of their time is spent scurrying around the desert, practising Ninja techniques with other men. When not practising, they sit around the camp-fire meditating silently. Before he joined the Ninjas, Ootsie used to frequent Big Mary's, and I guess the sight of females has stirred some memories.

I wonder if they might be getting stirred a little too much, as he now seems to be standing extremely close to Sub Girl. Were it not forbidden to Wasteland Ninjas,

I'd say he was admiring her. A poor choice, I can but feel. Okay, Sub Girl is attractive enough if you like that sort of thing – all leather clothes, the sides of her head shaved and her hair tied back with a red ribbon – but she's a thug of the worst order, almost as bad as Tank Girl.

'What a pretty ribbon,' mutters Ootsie, but so softly that no one but me hears it, which is just as well, as the Wasteland Ninjas are deadly enemies of Tank Girl and all her companions. Any Ninja paying a compliment to one of them is liable to get lynched.

15

Half an hour later Alvin finishes his first set. It has been
a difficult half-hour for me, involving losing a lot of
money and drinking a lot of beer. Since the terrible
news about the *Venus de Milo* I have been unable to
concentrate and have not won a hand. My head is
muddled and my money is almost exhausted. Tank
Girl, Sub Girl and Wanda the Gun Dealer are still
figuring strongly, but myself, the Professor, Mining Jim
and Jet Girl are all showing signs of fading, as are
Booga and Donner, the two stupid kangaroos.

I am deeply tired, and more than once I feel like
giving up altogether, but there are several important
reasons I have to keep playing. For one thing, I have a
reputation as a champion drinker to maintain, and I
utterly refuse to let anyone outdrink me, although I
have to admit that Tank Girl is doing a good job of it
so far. For another, I want the 200-zoobie prize, plus
table winnings, that comes to the last player left in the
game. And for another, I've placed a huge bet on
myself to win with ZugZug the Bookmaker and I am
unable to actually meet this bet if I lose. Naturally, to
survive as a bookmaker in the Wastelands, ZugZug is a
violent thug, and she has plenty of collectors, always
ready to do terrible things to defaulters.

There are way too many violent and terrible people in
the Wastelands. Sometimes I think I should pack it all
in and go and live quietly as a clerk in Lugit City.

Of course, if I was to make it up to Lugit with the

Venus de Milo I could sell it for millions of zoobies, and all my problems would be solved. How to get it back from the Shaolin Queens, though, that's the problem. No solution presents itself, but thinking about the *Venus de Milo* does give me a sudden inspiration as to how to raise some more money and stay in the game. I'll sell it again. Of course, it already belongs to Magdalen but, when I win the game, I'll be able to pay back whoever else I've palmed it off on.

This seems like an excellent plan. You must remember, I have now been drinking for nearly thirty hours.

As Alvin's electronic thunder comes to an end, Tank Girl wastes no time in picking up her story where she left off.

'So there we were, shagged by fate once more,' she says. 'Little Wee Sam in the hands of Water and Power, and this time taken to their headquarters, where she would be heavily guarded by whole armies of soldiers, and tanks and rockets and things. As you will all be aware, I'm not a woman to shirk my moral responsibilities, and felt that it was my duty to rescue her. So some weeks later, when our beer ran out, I got round to thinking of a plan.

'What we need, I said to Jet Girl, is a bit of outside help. We should recruit an army and just barrel down on Water and Power headquarters and wipe them out once and for all. I mean, they deserve it. I'm sick of them always trying to spoil my fun. You can't go out for a drink and a curry without a squadron of their soldiers turning up and spoiling things, and then, by the time you've wiped out the soldiers and washed the blood off your hands, your rice has gone cold. And now they've gone and kidnapped young – what was her name? – Sam, that's it, now they've gone and kidnapped young Sam and are no doubt inflicting countless torments on her. You know that Kesslee person likes to quote poetry at his victims? The man's a monster. No mercy at all. I've had enough. It's time to consign Water and Power to the ashcan of history.'

The kangaroos cheer. Dumb beasts.

'Jet Girl was in full agreement, but she didn't see where we could recruit an army. It was then I revealed what may well go down in history as one of the finest military manoeuvres yet conceived, which was to recruit the Rippers.'

The Kangaroos cheer again. Have you ever heard a kangaroo cheer? It's not pleasant.

'Yes!' roars Tank Girl, pounding her fist on the table. 'The Rippers! Those mysterious, powerful, seldom seen, yet implacable enemies of Water and Power, who alone held the area around the Blue Dunes free from tyranny, always turning up where they were least expected and mangling a few troops. "Recruit the Rippers and we'll be all right," I said. "We'll tear down the walls of Water and Power headquarters and set my people free. And if any of them are nice-looking we might get a good shag out of it as well." Because I have to admit that the Wastelands in those days were fairly short of opportunities for sex, being mainly populated by crazed hermits, radiation mutants and suchlike. Ever since wandering into the upstairs rooms at the Liquid Silver Bordello, my lack of a sex-life had been on my mind a little, but the crazed hermits and radiation mutants just weren't suitable. Bits kept falling off them at the wrong time. Not erotic at all.

'Jet Girl was frightened of approaching the Rippers –'

'No, I wasn't,' interrupts Jet Girl.

'Yes, you were,' says Tank Girl.

'I was not.'

'You were scared shitless.'

'That's a lie.'

Play is interrupted by a brief argument.

'Jet Girl was moderately nervous of approaching the Rippers,' continues Tank Girl after a while. 'I was quite looking forward to it. They had a reputation as ferocious and psychopathic killers. My sort of people, really.

'So I got into the trusty tank, revved it up, fired a few shells into the Old Orphanage, or New Orphanage as it was then, just to get my aim in, and set off.

'We headed back to the place where the Water and Power soldiers had taken us before, the subgate or whatever it was, and walked straight in. Jet Girl, who is, I have to admit, a bit of a technical wizard, had built a special "Ripper Detector Meter" to let us know when they were about but it went wrong after I poured some beer over it, so after we'd gone down the subgate we just walked along the mineshaft shouting "Yoohoo, where are you?" and "any deadly Rippers here?" and that sort of thing for a while, and what do you know? Some Rippers appeared. I've always felt that life is simple if you just get directly to the point. Don't muck around, that's what I say. No point prevaricating. If you want a Ripper, just go and ask for one.'

At this point Tank Girl is so wrapped up in her own story that she fails to notice a trick, and the Professor scoops it up. Tank Girl snaps her fingers as if she doesn't care and carries on talking.

'I expect you want to know what the Rippers were like?'

'No,' say Mining Jim, the Professor, Wanda the Gun Dealer and me.

'They were ugly as hell,' says Tank Girl, ignoring us. 'I mean, *ugly*. *Really* ugly. Big claws and wiry hair. Not much prospect of a shag here, I thought to myself, but they look strong and, under my brilliant leadership, may well be capable of storming the headquarters of Water and Power, vast, strong and technologically advanced as it is.

'I was just about to put this to them, when I saw that they were under a few misapprehensions. For one thing, they thought we'd come to attack them and, for another, they thought they'd captured us. We were standing round discussing this for a while – who had actually captured who and suchlike – and they were looking threatening, and one of them even wanted to kill us, and I was just starting to think that maybe instead of recruiting them I should just hand out a few severe slappings, when the tunnels suddenly started to fill up with gas. It was their defence mechanism, activated by the presence of humans.

' "Oh no, we're doomed!" cried Jet Girl.'

'No, I did not,' protests Jet Girl, not looking very pleased.

'Yes, you did. Or something to that effect, anyway. I was just getting ready to leg it out of the tunnel, when I realized the smell was one I recognized. It was laughing-gas. The Rippers had hooked up a big vat of the stuff to the tunnel. So there we were: me, Jet Girl, and eight deadly Rippers all rolling about laughing like we were old friends. Broke the ice completely, and they invited us to tea.'

'T-Saint didn't want to invite you,' remarks Booga, glancing at the large unconscious kangaroo in the corner.

'No, he didn't. He was mean in those days. Couldn't hold his drink then either. But apart from T-Saint, everyone else seemed pleased enough to see us. And when the Rippers took their body armour and helmets off they didn't look so bad, and were in fact these cuddly kangaroos you see here now.

'And you know what happened after that?' says Tank Girl.

'What?'

'*Snap!*' she says, and rakes in her winnings, looking pleased with herself.

16

A fight breaks out at the pinball table between a young Post-Apocalypse Biker Girl and one of the Wasteland Ninjas. A few others run over to join in, but it is all brought to a sudden halt when Loretta Dragon Slayer steps up and knocks everyone around the pinball table flying, with what seems like the slightest touch of her arm. I think this is because she does not want any violence to disturb her boss, John the Brute, rather than any desire on her part to play pinball. I could be wrong. The most unlikely people can get quite fanatical about pinball.

There are five or six bruised bodies now hauling themselves to their feet in the far corner.

'An impressive début for Loretta Dragon Slayer,' says the Professor.

There are some mutters of agreement around the table, but Tank Girl sneers loudly.

'Loretta Dragon Fucker,' she mocks. 'Couldn't fight her way out of a soggy cornflake packet.'

'She's the Kung Fu champion of the continent.'

Tank Girl spits on the floor.

'Bollocks.'

She glances over at me.

'What's this about 1,000,000 zoobies, Trader?'

I make no reply, and hope that Tank Girl does not choose to get involved in the *Venus de Milo* affair. *Venus* is still sitting in the dark corner in her baseball cap and combat jacket, the serenest figure in the place.

'You could do with a few zoobies,' she says to me, mockingly. 'You've hardly got enough for your stake.'

'I have means of raising funds, Tank Girl.'

Which is what I set out to do. I hunt out Eldrich San and draw him to one side.

'Eldrich San. I have with me an immensely valuable work of art. Worth upwards of 1,000,000 zoobies. Its like will never be offered for sale again, and collectors in Lugit City will kill to buy it. And, as you've always been a good friend to me, I will let you have it for 1,000 zoobies, provided you can pay me right now.'

Eldrich San does not look impressed. He is not impolite, but does intimate that he finds this a little hard to believe.

'Really, it's true. Go and ask the Professor. You know he is an expert on everything and is completely trustworthy. But be discreet. Don't let anyone know about it – I don't want to start a riot.'

One thing about Eldrich San; he doesn't waste time. Ninja training, I suppose. He makes his way over to the Professor and whispers in his ear. He returns a few minutes later.

'Well, Trader, it seems to be true. The statue is as valuable as you say. But why, I wonder, are you selling it for 1,000 zoobies?'

I decide that honesty will serve me best and admit to Eldrich San that I need money to stay in the game.

'Gambling is for fools,' he says. 'Wait here.'

Eldrich San might disapprove of gambling, but he is obviously not averse to making a healthy profit, because he immediately goes to see how much money he can raise from the other Wasteland Ninjas. He returns with a small bag.

'600 zoobies,' he says. 'All I can raise at such short notice.'

'I'll take it.'

I grab it, because it is time for the game to start again.

'One thing,' I say to Eldrich San before taking my leave, 'don't mention this to anyone else. You can imagine what would happen in this den of thieves if word got out about 1,000,000-zoobie artwork. Just leave the statue where it is, and you can remove it discreetly at the end.'

I am well pleased with myself. I am now able to remain in the game. There may be a little trouble later, when both Eldrich San and Magdalen claim ownership, but no doubt I'll be able to sort it out. When I win the game, I'll be rich. Everything will be fine.

Play continues. After the next round there is a surprise withdrawal. Wanda the Gun Dealer had seemed to be going well but abruptly she pushes away her beer. 'To hell with it,' she growls, face going green. 'I quit.'

She stumbles away with the help of a few of her employees and the pile of money in front of her is pushed into the pot in the middle. This means that the next hand is a very valuable one.

Now left in the game are Tank Girl, Jet Girl, Sub Girl, Mining Jim, the Professor and me. Naturally, many of the people in the bar have been placing bets on the eventual winner all through the game, but the betting reaches a new frenzy as Wanda quits the scene and ZugZug the Bookmaker enters the bar.

As the door swings open, there is the customary blast of howling wind and freezing rain; then, it's back to normal, except that the throng of people in Big Mary's place now includes ZugZug and her paid protectors, the Children of the Temple of the Sun.

The Children of the Temple of the Sun have shaved heads, yellow robes and pockets full of religious tracts. Usually, their hands are full of big plasma-blasting rifles, presumably for chastising heretics and blasphemers, but for now they've checked them in at the door. They wander around the desert chanting all the time, which is really irritating and, in between doing that, they hire themselves out to ZugZug as her protectors when she needs protecting, which is quite often, as a successful bookmaker can make a lot of enemies.

I am less than thrilled at their presence. When placing my bet with ZugZug, I had rather thought that she would not actually be here. I was intending to call in at her office next day if I'd won, and disappear without seeing her if I'd lost. Her arrival is very bad news.

ZugZug is no more than average size and, with her short brown hair and her scruffy denim jacket, rather anonymous-looking among the exotic inhabitants of Big Mary's, but she is extremely quick on the draw and has never in the past shown any hesitation about killing anyone defaulting on a bet. Or getting the Children of the Temple of the Sun to do it for her.

She will have checked her gun in with the doorman, and I wonder about the chances of fleeing to the newly supercharged Big Trader Truck and disappearing over the horizon before she could reclaim it. But this is defeatism. I'll win the game and everything will be fine. No need to disappear over the horizon, just rake in the cash from all sides and stroll off into the sunset.

ZugZug immediately comes up to see how play is

progressing, while the Children take bets round the bar.

'Still in the running, Trader?' she asks. 'Good for you. I take it you have the 500 zoobies ready to pay me if you lose?'

Tank Girl bursts out laughing.

'The Trader bet 500 zoobies on himself to win the game?'

'And why not?' I demand. 'I'm still here, aren't I?'

'Not for long, Trader. Drink up!'

Tank Girl downs another beer, although it is not the end of a round.

'Not till I have to,' I say, rather lamely, and she laughs again, along with the kangaroos. How I hate these kangaroos. You can't convince me they're Genetically Engineered Super Soldiers.

'So, it turned out that the kangaroos were Genetically Engineered Super Soldiers,' says Tank Girl. 'Designed by the fabled Johnny Prophet. They were meant to be working for Water and Power but had departed from the scene when Johnny Prophet went missing. They were carrying on a guerilla war against Kesslee and were doing quite well at it, what with their genetic super-strength and their special body armour. They kept massacring patrols and pillaging isolated outposts of Water and Power, which was very bad for morale. Kesslee, as I mentioned earlier, was furious.

'However, the Rippers weren't making what I would have called real progress, and I quickly convinced them that what they needed most was a brilliant general to lead them to ultimate victory. Fortunately for them, that person had now arrived in the shape of Tank Girl, world-renowned as a brilliant general and famous for her capacity for beer.'

She drinks again. It is surprising that she never seems to put on weight.

'I told them about a few of my famous battles, such as my victory at Liquid Silver and my stunning defeat of a squadron of tanks that sneaked up on me one time, when I was having my afternoon nap. A disgraceful thing to do, for which I repaid them with a crushing barrage of fire, driving my tank up and down mountains with one hand and throwing rocks with the other. They couldn't deal with this sort of thing and retreated as fast as they could. I followed them and annihilated the whole squadron, and still had time to finish my nap.

'And then there was the time when fourteen huge jets sent by Kesslee started dive-bombing me when I was having my breakfast by the camp-fire. I was trapped out in the open but I just loaded up my catapult with sugar lumps and fired at their engines, and they started tumbling out of the sky, engines jammed up with sticky goo. Pilots were bailing out everywhere, so I got some good boomerang practice in. I hit three parachutists with one throw, and the boomerang still came back to me. Afterwards my tank was in a bad mood because I'd won the battle without him, so I had to be extra nice to him and take him to the toyshop to buy him a *Thomas the Tank Engine* book, which is his favourite. And all this was before breakfast!

'Well, of course, when they heard about these famous victories, the Rippers couldn't help being impressed. Awestruck, really.'

'*Fabula etiamsi falsa lepida est*,' mutters the Professor, which he tells me afterwards roughly translates as, these stories are all total lies but you have to admit she tells them well.

Tank Girl continues.

'"Let's go and do it!" I cried, and made ready to leap into my tank and completely trash Water and Power headquarters. But the Rippers still hung back. Not because they were shy or anything, just scaredy-cats.'

'I wasn't a scaredy-cat,' protests Donner.

'Yes, you were,' say Tank Girl and Jet Girl simultaneously. Donner looks suitably abashed.

'It was only natural to exhibit a little caution,' he says.

'Pah!' Tank Girl snorts. 'I never exhibit caution. Caution is for wimps and kangaroos. Caution sucks, that's what I say. I was all for driving straight up there and giving them hell, but the Rippers seemed to suspect we might be leading them into a trap. T-Saint, who was big and mean and seemed to be in charge, was still very dubious about the whole thing, so, eventually, me and Jet Girl said we'd go and do a little preparatory work that would show them what a safe bet it was to side with Tank Girl.

'Donner, who was their technical genius, or as close to a technical genius as a Genetically Engineered kangaroo can get, which is not all that close when it comes right down to it, had discovered that a new cargo of weapons was due in at the Water and Power storage depot.

'"Say no more," I declared. "Myself and Jet Girl will go and remove that cargo of arms. Once you see the cool way we go about things you'll be only too happy to march under the Tank Girl banner."

'So off we went. I seem to remember meeting Sub Girl again sometime around here, but if I did, all she would have said was "the rains are coming" or "*après moi le déluge*" or some similarly dumb thing, so I won't dwell on the incident.'

I glance at Sub Girl, but, as usual, she is paying no attention to Tank Girl's ramblings, preferring instead to keep her attention on the game. I notice, however, that Ootsie, the young Wasteland Ninja, is standing by her elbow with a stupid expression on his face, and I wonder why he is not over with his friend Bitsy at the pool-table.

The atmosphere around the table is now extremely tense because there is a very large pot to be won, containing all the money that Wanda had in front of her before she quit. Whoever wins this hand will be sure to survive in the game for some time. As there are various players whose reserves are low, there is a lot to play for. I try and concentrate as hard as I can, but Tank Girl's diatribe is having the desired effect on me and several others, and putting us off our game. A three of hearts is played on top of a three of spades. There is a general cry of *snap!* and many hands pound down on the table, but the bottom-most hand is found to be that of Sub Girl. The Underwater Mistress of the Depths has got there first and rakes in the huge pile of money.

'Well done, Sub Girl,' says Tank Girl, pretending she doesn't care, and drinks her beer down in a second. It takes me ages to force mine down, and I feel like I'm positively drowning in the stuff. Out of the corner of my eye I notice ZugZug looking hard at me, and I groan inside. It is a great relief when Big Mary comes over and announces it is time for the next break, and I can go and empty myself of some of the beer in the toilet and try to get back to being human again.

17

The Four Dwarfs, gruesome guardians of John the Brute, are in the toilet. Presumably they do everything together.

'Well, look who it is.'

'The Trader.'

'Would that be the Trader who –'

'– swindled John the Brute?'

I protest my innocence.

'I did not swindle him. There was merely a little confusion over accountancy practices – a common occurrence in complicated business deals.'

'Getting chopped up is a common occurrence in business deals where we come from,' one of them says, caressing his axe.

Another threat. Once more I deeply regret ever coming to Big Mary's Bar and Grill to play in the Annual Wastelands Snap and Drinking Competition. Sheer bravado on my part, thinking it would be good for my reputation to emerge as the Wasteland's best drinker and card-player. Now, I am more concerned with simply emerging.

I am losing count of how many people there are in the bar who a) *could* kill me and b) may want to do so before the day is over. It is a depressingly long list.

'Well,' I tell the dwarfs. 'John the Brute, esteemed Bandit King of the Red Mountains, may possibly have intimated to you that there was a slight misunderstanding over the arms deal. But surely it cannot have escaped your notice how keen he is to do business with me again? Why, he's come all the way from the Red Mountains to purchase an important work of art from me.'

The dwarfs chuckle.

'Purchase? Who said anything about purchase? John the Brute doesn't purchase works of art from slimy little traders. John the Brute takes what he wants from them, and we chop them up if they object.'

Well, you can't say fairer than that.

They leave. I rid myself of a few gallons of beer and meditate morosely on what I've just heard. Unfortunately the dwarfs were speaking the truth. I realize that I was fairly foolish even to think that John the Brute would do a fair deal with me. Even if it was mine to sell, he would just take the statue and depart, most probably leaving me in several pieces. If I don't manage to get it back from Magdalen, he'll probably just chop me up anyway. Curse the stupid statue! Why did it want to go and get uncovered by a sand-storm just before I drove by in the trusty Big Trader Truck? For a moment everything seems hopeless and I feel like giving up the fight.

But, you know, standing there in the toilet, my hopes revive a little. My spirit is not so easily vanquished. The Trader, people have been known to say, is not a man whose spirit is easily vanquished. Put him in a tight situation and he is entirely likely to show his true mettle and squirm out of it somehow. I start to think about how I might squirm out of this one, and show a small profit as well.

As I'm leaving, Ootsie the Wasteland Ninja comes in, the same dumb look still on his face. I give him a friendly greeting, as he is a nice young guy, but he brushes aside my small-talk and utters a few miscellaneous sounds of rapture.

'Isn't she wonderful?' he breathes.

'Who?'

'Sub Girl, of course.'

'No,' I say.

'You're an idiot, Trader. Sub Girl is the most divine creature ever to walk the face of the earth. Or sail under it.'

I stare at him, amazed. Were it not for the fact that the Wasteland Ninjas are notorious non-drinkers, I would say he was drunk. Divine creature? Sub Girl? The one who goes around wrecking things with her submarine and prophesying doom and disaster? The man is a fool.

It's all too much for me. I leave him combing his blue hair and hurry out of the toilet. Right outside is Eldrich San.

'Ah, Eldrich San. You must be eager to take delivery of the *Kung Fu* videos, each one featuring the venerable David Carradine, ancient hero of your sect.'

Eldrich San waves his hand dismissively.

'Never mind the *Kung Fu* videos,' he says. 'When can we have the statue?'

'Immediately after the game, as agreed. You know I can't leave before then.'

He seems to accept this, and I hurry by. I bang into a solid phalanx of Shaolin Queens.

'Just the women I was looking for!' I exclaim. 'Magdalen, a confidential word with you. Due to a favourable business transaction, my financial situation has taken an upturn, and I am pleased to announce that I can pay you thirty-five zoobies for the statue which you only recently purchased for twenty-five. A solid profit of ten zoobies. How about it?'

Magdalen shakes her head.

'Okay Magdalen, I can see you are experienced in business matters. I'll make it forty.'

Again she shakes her head.

'Well, why not? It's only an old statue.'

'It may be only an old statue to you. To us it is the new representation of our Goddess. Our last one was destroyed by an earthquake and it is obvious to us that this one has been sent to us from above. It is not for sale at any price. 'Bye Trader.'

She leaves. I curse. Dumb Shaolin Queens. You sell them a cheap statue, and they immediately start worshipping it. Doesn't make sense. Now how am I going to get it back and sell it to John the Brute for a vast profit? I have no idea but I don't give up hope. At least the Shaolin Queens don't know its true value.

I turn round and bang into Bitsy, second of the young Ninja recruits and also quite a nice guy.

'What are you doing, standing right behind me?' I complain.

He doesn't reply immediately. There is something familiar about the dumb expression on his face.

'Isn't she wonderful?' he says, after a while.

'Who?'

'Who? Magdalen, of course. Who else?'

'Magdalen? You're joking.'

Bitsy looks offended.

'I do not joke about the woman I love.'

'Oh, come on, you can't love Magdalen. She's a thug and, anyway, the Shaolin Queens are your enemies.'

'How dare you insult her,' says Bitsy. 'She is divine: I worship her.'

This is, again, too much for me, and I hurry away. That's the problem with these young Wasteland Ninjas. You march them over the desert pretending to be palm trees for months on end and they never see a woman and then, when they come somewhere like Big Mary's Bar and Grill, they can't cope. They start falling in love with utterly unsuitable women like Sub Girl and Magdalen. This Ninja lifestyle must be unhealthy. I mean, it can't be good for them, all this wandering around the desert continually disguising themselves as rocks and things. I'll have to have a word with Eldrich San about it.

Loretta Dragon Slayer hoves into view. She waves me over. I depart in the opposite direction. I crash into ZugZug. She glares at me and calls me a drunken oaf. I hurry back to the game. It might be hard work at the card-table, drinking endless beers and listening to Tank Girl's dull stories, but it's beginning to seem like a haven of peace compared to the rest of the bar.

18

From the way the Children of the Temple of the Sun are studying me as I struggle through the crowd back to the table, I would say that the general odds on me winning the competition are not high.

Of all the many gangs, sects and private armies that wander the deserts of the Wastelands, I think I dislike the Children of the Temple of the Sun the most. For one thing, they look stupid in their yellow robes and, for another, they are always chanting some peculiar thing in a language I don't understand, and it just annoys me. Furthermore, they claim to be ascetics so they never buy anything from me, and I have little time for anyone who never buys anything from me.

How come, I wonder, if they are so ascetic and religious, they are prepared to hire themselves out to ZugZug as protectors? Yes sir, the Children of the Temple of the Sun are the worst. But, there again, the Post-Apocalypse Biker Girls are pretty bad as well when it comes right down to it, always racing around the desert on their motorbikes whacked out of their heads on hallucinogens, shooting guns everywhere and generally being a menace to society and feuding with the Post-Apocalypse Biker Boys who are, meanwhile, racing around the desert on their motorbikes, whacked out of their heads on hallucinogens, shooting guns everywhere and generally being a menace to society. Really, it can be a hard task just to innocently cross the Wastelands without some gang of delinquent bikers poking a gun in your face and rambling on about pink rabbits and talking cacti and 'have you seen how beautiful everything looks today?' And if that isn't bad enough, then it's the Shaolin Queens of the Desert, marching over the dunes practising their Kung Fu techniques on anyone who gets in the way, and the Wasteland Ninjas hanging around practising their ninja techniques by pretending to be palm trees and leaping out and scaring passers-by with blood-curdling yells and terrifying poses. And then there's Tank Girl and her cronies, always roaming around with huge crates of beer strapped to their vehicles and being about as objectionable as a bunch of people possibly can be. I don't even want to think about the mayhem they cause on a day-to-day basis. It's getting so a man can't do an honest day's work without some group of maniacs harassing him in some way or other. I hate them all. Something should be done about it. The government should send more soldiers to the Wastelands and bring a little peace and quiet back to the area. More discipline, that's what we need around here.

Feeling rather grumpy, I rejoin the game. The cards are dealt.

'Where was I?' asks Tank Girl.

'In the toilet,' says Booga, quite seriously.

Tank Girl drums her fingers on the table. Even she finds Booga hard to take sometimes.

'Carrying out a scouting mission to the Water and Power storage depot,' says Jet Girl.

'So we were. The storage depot. The Rippers fixed us up with some mobile cameras so they could see what we were doing, and we went off to scout out the dump. It turned out to be quite a simple affair. Myself and Jet

Girl just waltzed in, dripping with glamour – we'd power-dressed for the occasion – and told the guards we'd come to shoot a documentary: *A Day in the Life of a Water and Power Minion*. Then we took some pictures and waltzed out again. Easy.'

'You missed out a bit,' Jet Girl says.

'Did I? Oh, you mean the bit where they didn't believe a word of our story and turned the full firepower of their weapons on us in an attempt to blow us off the face of the earth? Didn't seem worth mentioning. It all came to the same thing in the end: we departed with pictures of their new weapons and went back to Ripper HQ to plan the raid.'

'What was the point of this scouting mission?' asks the Professor, puzzled. 'Given that the Rippers, through Donner's technology, already had pictures of the storage depot?'

'Beats me,' says Tank Girl. 'I never understood it myself, but I was off my head on laughing-gas.'

Play heats up and the cards come down fast from all the players. It seems like a long time since I've won a hand and I'm feeling pressurized. Once your money's gone, you're out, even if you haven't succumbed to the effects of the alcohol. Eyeing the pile of money in front of me makes me wonder anxiously about ZugZug. The zoobies I got from Eldrich San are disappearing fast. I would try and cheat again, but I know Tank Girl is keeping a sharp eye on me. I concentrate as hard as I can, trying to follow the cards, despite Tank Girl's despicable diversionary tactics.

'So,' she announces. 'It was time for some real action at last. Water and Power had ruled the continent unchallenged since the comet blew away civilization as we knew it, and we were now going to wipe them out, or at the very least give them a hard time. First task was to steal a bundle of weapons from the dump, then, it was straight on to their headquarters to rescue Sam and stick a rocket right up Kesslee's ass. Without the assistance of lubrication, if I was feeling mean.

'Donner got some pictures through on his scanner. A huge convoy was leaving the storage depot. Now was our moment. I loaded up my tank, Jet Girl loaded up her jet and the Rippers put on their body armour. "Battle stations!" I cried. "All hands on deck! Give 'em hell! I regret I have but one life to give to my country!" And with more exhortations like these to cheer up the troops I led us into battle.

'We drove over the desert, which was a real desert in those days. None of your rain for forty days and forty nights like we have now: it was baked solid and hardly a palm tree in sight. Using the tactical skills I'd developed when tracking down buffalos as a child we soon came upon the convoy.'

Tank Girl stands up and starts waving her arms about, although we are still playing cards.

'"Forward!" I cried. "Attack! Kill them all! Let no one escape! Geronimo!" And in we went! A tidal wave of unstoppable force, human and kangaroo warriors fighting for the freedom of the planet, linked together, unstoppable, irresistible –'

'It was a shame we were attacking a peaceful gypsy convoy,' says Jet Girl.

Tank Girl sits down.

'Yes, that did spoil it a bit. The gypsies were pretty mad afterwards. Those of them left alive. But, as I explained to them at the time, those are the fortunes of war. Innocent civilians will get hurt. It's all for the greater good of humanity. Mind you, later on I couldn't understand how we'd mistaken their horsedrawn wagons for an armoured military convoy. Just carried away with enthusiasm, I suppose.

'After that we spent ages looking for the right convoy. Took us hours. I was dying for a beer. When we eventually found them I'd kind of lost interest, couldn't seem to work up the enthusiasm to shout "Geronimo" and suchlike any more, so we just attacked them quietly. Bit of an anticlimax really, just wiping them out and taking their weapons.'

'But I saved your life, Tank Girl,' says Booga. 'That wasn't an anticlimax.'

Tank Girl yawns.

'Don't give us that old story again, Booga. You didn't save my life. I was perfectly in command of the situation. Okay, I jumped on top of a truck when it was racing out of control with no brakes and speeding towards a cliff, but I was *enjoying* it. I like that sort of thing. I was going to ride it down the cliff like a surfboard. I admit you did demonstrate your Genetically Engineered Super-speed and strength when you stopped the truck with your bare hands, but it was quite unnecessary. I was well in control. I'm always well in control.'

Booga looks down, disappointed that his hero has refused to acknowledge that he saved her life. This works out well for Booga, however, because just as he looks down, a five is played on top of a five and he shouts *snap!* before anyone else notices.

I curse. My pile of money is now smaller than ever. A

hand grips my shoulder. I turn round. It's Iris Grim, leader of the Post-Apocalypse Biker Girls.

'How much for the statue, Trader?' she asks.

19

I'm unable to reply to Iris Grim, as further conversation becomes impossible when Alvin and his band swagger back onstage to play their second set. After some hours of partying in Big Mary's, they are a little unsteady on their feet. Alvin's make-up is running in the heat. They wave to the audience in a grand manner copied from old videos I've sold them of stadium rock bands back in the pre-comet days, although Big Mary's Bar and Grill is about as far away from a stadium as you can get. Some of the politer rock bands in Lugit City refuse to play here at all, deeming it too much of a health risk.

Alvin has now plugged his instrument, which is some sort of unnamed electronic box, into the old fuzzbox. As they start up it makes a very impressive racket. It sounds quite unlike anything ever heard here before, that is to say, much more unpleasant, and this goes down well with the crowd.

I try to take stock of the situation. John the Brute, Bandit King of the Red Mountains, wants the *Venus de Milo* as a present for his lover. He knows its value but is unlikely to pay me anything. With the Four Dwarfs and Loretta Dragon Slayer on his side, he doesn't really need to. Even on his own he wouldn't really need to. Everyone says he is the strongest and most savage person on the continent and I believe it. For one thing, he is the only person who is unafraid to publicly abuse Tank Girl. He has often been heard to say that, if she ever cares to visit the Red Mountains, he will be happy to single-handedly ram her tank down her throat.

Unfortunately for John the Brute, and for me, I have already sold the *Venus de Milo* to the Shaolin Queens of the Desert. On their own I do not think they match up to John the Brute and his subordinates, but there are a lot of Shaolin Queens, and they have a powerful reason for wanting the statue: they regard it as a Goddess, more or less.

Unfortunately for the Shaolin Queens, and also for me, I have also sold the statue to the Wasteland Ninjas, who will no doubt be looking forward to selling it at an immense profit. Again, they are less formidable than John the Brute, but there are also a lot of them, and they are no pushovers. Furthermore, they are deadly rivals of the Shaolin Queens and would surely not let them have the statue without a fight.

Why did Iris Grim express an interest? Presumably, she too wants to make a profit. The Biker Girls, like the Biker Boys, are a strong gang, and scared of no one. Of course, I haven't actually sold it to Iris Grim yet. I don't have to sell it to her. I could avoid complicating my life like this. Still, eyeing my pile of money, which is again shrinking, I realize that I might have to. Why not? Might as well sell it three times as twice. I can pay everybody back when I win the game.

I think we have been drinking for over thirty-two hours now. Possibly, my thinking on this matter is not as clear as it might be. To hell with it – it's only a statue after all.

Then there are ZugZug the Bookmaker and the Children of the Temple of the Sun. So far they have not expressed any interest in the *Venus de Milo*, but they will have their own reason for wanting to do me violence if my luck at cards doesn't change quickly. This *Venus de Milo* affair has interfered with my first aim in coming here, which was to win the card-game and drinking contest, and I remember that even that may cause trouble. I'm convinced Tank Girl won't let me walk away with the prize, no matter what. She is a terrible loser. At least she's not involved in the statue business as yet. I wonder what sort of price she'd pay? She's no friend of mine. We have never had an actual dispute about anything but every time we meet she makes fun of me, and she knows I despise her.

Still, Tank Girl is pretty formidable herself . . . How would she stand up against John the Brute, I wonder? They really do hate each other.

Is there any way of getting Tank Girl on my side while still holding on to the statue? Allowing me to sell it in Lugit City for a vast profit? I can't think of one.

Tank Girl wins the next hand. The Professor rallies and wins the next. Jet Girl wins the next. My funds are now extremely low. Everything is going wrong. I consider flinging myself on the mercy of the admirable Jet Girl and begging her to take me away from all this in her jet. I don't expect she would. Donner is still hanging around her protectively. I hate him. I still wish I could come up with a good kebab joke.

20

Despite the noise coming from Alvin onstage, Tank Girl does not relent in her storytelling. She stands up, waves her arms about for effect and yells. She has a very loud voice, another of her bad points. Stentorian, the Professor calls it. What is the root cause of this continual desire to be the centre of attention? We wonder.

'Perhaps she was ignored as a child,' suggests the Professor.

'That's easy to believe. I wish I could ignore her as an adult.'

She rants on.

'So, after raiding the convoy and stealing loads of crates of weapons, it was back to the Ripper hide-out for some good solid partying and drinking. These poor suckers the Rippers, or "dumb kangaroos", as I had now learned to call them, challenged me to a drinking contest. They thought they could drink me under the table. Drink me under the table?'

She shakes with laughter.

'Drink? Did you ever meet a marsupial who could hold his beer? Me neither. Sad, really. A few gallons down the line they just come apart at the seams and start puking up and falling down unconscious – pitiful really, almost made me feel sorry for them – stumbling round pissed out of their heads with their tails getting in the way of their big feet. And they all got maudlin for Johnny Prophet, who created them in the first place and taught them everything they knew etcetera, before disappearing off on some secret mission or other years ago. They all got quite horny as well, which might possibly have been interesting, had they not all been totally incapable of getting it up after nine or ten gallons of beer. As a sad and pathetic sight, eight limp kangaroos takes some beating.'

Those kangaroos still awake at the table, Booga and Donner, look less than thrilled as Tank Girl shouts out details of their sexual failings so loudly, that even people on the far side of the room look over and laugh.

'Why kangaroos, anyway?' screams Tank Girl, going off on a tangent. 'Why not Genetically Engineered Wombats? I mean "wombat" is at least a funny word. You could get a laugh just at the mention of a Genetically Engineered Super Wombat. You could write a funny super-wombat song and sing it in the bath. You could write a comic and call it *Combat Wombat*.

'Or Koala bears, perhaps, bred to hang around looking cute in trees before leaping down on their opponents' necks and tearing them to pieces. No one would suspect a thing till it was too late.'

Tank Girl does her impersonation of a Genetically Engineered Super Koala Bear leaping down from a tree on to someone's neck. Chaos threatens at the card-table, and it becomes extremely difficult to play. Have you ever tried keeping your concentration on a fast and exacting card-game on which your life depends, whilst Tank Girl impersonates a killer Koala bear leaping from a tree? A dreadful experience, I can assure you.

The cards are thundering down on the table. Tank Girl keeps playing her hand while hanging upside down from the back of her chair and ranting about wombats and the sexual inadequacies of kangaroos, and all the while she is pouring beer down her throat and screaming at Big Mary to bring her a pizza, because she's feeling a little peckish. So, it is no surprise to me, given this sort of distraction, when I miss the next trick and the Professor scoops it up. Professors, I suppose, have better concentration than traders. And miners. Mining Jim is now out of money and out of the game. He shakes his head rather sadly and leaves the table.

'See what's happened to my pizza, will you?' shouts Tank Girl after him but he ignores her.

The situation is now serious for me. I have only enough left in front of me to stake myself in for two more rounds. If I do not win one of them, I too will be out of the game.

Tank Girl, well aware of this, does not let up in her antics. As she has the largest pile of money in front of her, she can afford to lose a few hands while driving out the weaker players.

She describes the party with the kangaroos after the raid, although the greater part of this description is merely an endless recitation of how much beer she drank and how drunk she was and how she was dancing on top of tables and generally being the life and soul of the place, and it is just about to drive me completely mad, when she suddenly announces that when they got round to opening the crates of weapons the next day they found them to be empty.

'No weapons at all. Just sand. Except for the last crate which contained the body of Johnny Prophet, guru of the kangaroos. It also contained Sam's necklace. Corpse and jewelry both presumably placed there by Kesslee and Water and Power.

'I immediately realized it was a set-up. Somehow, they'd been monitoring us all along. They knew we were going to attack the convoy, and they'd put sand in the crates instead of weapons. Kesslee was playing with us.

'Well, the kangaroos were all for giving up there and then. Here we were, all set to launch a powerful surprise attack on Water and Power headquarters with an excellent collection of new weapons, and all we had was sand. And it seemed likely that Water and Power knew exactly what we were doing. Plus, of course, the kangaroos were upset because their beloved Johnny Prophet was dead.

'"Oh no," they wailed, "Johnny is dead, our mentor is gone, snatched from his secret mission and murdered by Kesslee." Their spirit was close to breaking, but I rallied the troops with a stirring speech.

'"Kangaroos," I said. "Stop hanging around like a bunch of softies and get ready to attack."

'"But we have no weapons, Tank Girl," they protested

'"We've got a tank and a jet," I told them. "And me, Tank Girl, undefeated champion of the universe. What more do you want?" This lifted their spirits.

'"And remember," I said. "My young friend Sam, an innocent ten-year-old, is in the clutches of Kesslee. Who knows what tortures he is inflicting on her at this very moment? We really should rescue her without delay."

'So, pausing only to drink the last crates of beer, cook a decent breakfast, sing a few songs, get the party going again, dance the night away and catch up with a few odd jobs that needed doing around the house, we set off some weeks later to rescue Sam and bring to an end once and for all the tyrannous domination of Kes-slee over the suffering continent.'

The kangaroos burst into applause.

'You are too kind,' says Tank Girl. 'Mind you, it was a fabulous performance on my part. Cheered the kangaroos up no end. I seem to remember we met Sub Girl some time around here and she was going on about the rains coming as she normally did, except she seemed more fervent than usual. She was a terrible bore in those days.'

Sub Girl does not react to this. Nor does her concentration on the game waver. I try to follow her example. Behind her, Ootsie continues to stare at her with some devotion. Idiot.

Donner is trying to put his arm around Jet Girl. I hate him. There must be a good kebab joke in his name somewhere.

'And that was it,' Tank Girl says. 'I had successfully rallied the troops. We were off, full speed ahead, ready to carry out the final attack on Water and Power.'

The kangaroos cheer again.

Two queens are played rapidly one after another. I see it happening but I react too slowly. First hand down on the pile is Sub Girl's. Damn it!

21

Sub Girl's victory coincides with the end of Alvin's set. Big Mary bustles up and announces a break. Before I can stretch my legs, a disconsolate young Ninja sits down beside me. It is Bitsy.

'I tried speaking to Magdalen,' he whispers in my ear. 'But she was extremely rude to me. I think I have made a mistake.'

I'm relieved to hear this. One, at least, of the two youthful lovers has come quickly to his senses. I wonder if Ootsie might have come to his? Glancing round I see that he apparently has not. He is crouching down by Sub Girl's chair, congratulating her on her success. In his enthusiasm he forgets to lower his voice.

'You were magnificent, Sub Girl.'

She looks at him with suspicion.

'Pardon?'

'The way you called *snap!* and got your hand down first. It was thrilling.'

Sub Girl has been drinking for thirty-five hours and feels some confusion.

'How was it thrilling?'

'They way you did it.'

'Did what?'

Now Ootsie looks confused. Sub Girl is not making things easy for him. He tries a different tactic.

'Can I buy you a drink?'

Sub Girl gives him a hostile stare.

'Are you completely out of your mind? I've been

sitting here for thirty-five hours forcing down one beer after another till I feel like a walking bag of vomit, and you want to buy me a drink? What's the matter with you? Are you trying to kill me?'

Ootsie looks distraught. His problem, of course, is that he has got a terrible crush on Sub Girl and he doesn't know what to do about it. It is a contingency not covered in his Ninja training. At stealing silently into an enemy fortress to assassinate an opponent, he's fine. At hanging around in the desert disguised as a palm tree, he has few equals. But put a woman he's attracted to in front of him, and he just goes to pieces. Hopeless really.

He realizes that things are not going very well. Sub Girl shows no signs of reacting favourably to him. Ootsie tries to work the conversation round till he can come out with something romantic but, even in this simple endeavour, he is hampered, because he is embarrassed by anything romantic. He is reticent in case Sub Girl makes fun of him. Also, he is extremely shy, and terrified of anyone else hearing his clumsy approaches.

There is an awkward silence.

'Perhaps I could bring you a pizza,' Ootsie eventually whispers in her ear.

'Hey, listen to this!' screams Tank Girl, appearing beside them. 'Young Ootsie's got the hots for Sub Girl. He's offering to bring her a pizza! Watch out for him, Sub Girl, these Wasteland Ninjas are terrible people. One bite of his pizza and he'll have your pants down. Hey Booga, listen to this, Ootsie wants to shag Sub Girl!'

Tank Girl and Booga cackle gleefully, and round the table everyone smiles. Sub Girl looks perplexed. Ootsie looks distraught, and flees.

'Bring me a pepperoni and mushroom and I'll let you feel my tits!' shouts Tank Girl at the retreating figure.

She turns to Booga.

'I always like to encourage young love. Didn't interrupt anything, did I, Sub Girl?'

There is more laughter around the table. Even though I feel sorry for Ootsie I can't prevent myself from turning to Bitsy with a grin.

'See what happens to young suitors?' I say.

He does not reply. On his face there is a familiar expression.

'Isn't she wonderful?' he breathes. 'So strong.'

'Who is?' I ask, puzzled.

'Tank Girl,' he says. 'I love her.'

'Don't be ridiculous,' I hiss at him. 'Tank Girl is a brute. She'd chop you into pieces.'

'Don't insult the woman I love,' he hisses back.

'What do you mean, "the woman you love"? Only five minutes ago you were in love with Magdalen.'

'A mere childish whim,' replies Bitsy. 'This is the real thing.'

22

Apart from the appalling Tank Girl, no one at the table finds it easy to swallow their beer. The other players, that is, Jet Girl, Sub Girl, Booga, Donner, the Professor and myself, all have great difficulty getting it down. It takes me a strong effort of will to finish my glass and I have the distinct impression that alcohol is now dribbling out of my ears. Booga seems to find it even harder. The instant he finishes his glass he puts his hands, or paws, over his mouth and stumbles away in the direction of the bathroom. From the way he crashes into the wall and ends up crawling on his belly under the pool-table I'd say he might not be coming back.

Well, one less player in the game brings me one step closer to victory, and I have the impression that Jet Girl may not be able to keep it up much longer either; but even though I feel just about able to cope with more drinking, I will be out of the game if my money runs out. As I have only the stake for one more round and have not won for ages, this may be very soon.

I leave Bitsy gazing at Tank Girl and wander away, trying to think of some way out of this predicament. Unfortunately, I do not look where I am going and I bump right into ZugZug.

'Got the 500 zoobies you owe me, Trader?'

I draw myself up to my full height. I feel sick. I shrink back down to normal.

'I don't owe you 500 zoobies, ZugZug.'

'You will after the next hand.'

'When and if I am forced to retire from the game, you may depend on being paid in full.'

ZugZug's mouth twitches. Possibly she imagines she is smiling. I notice that various members of the Children of the Temple of the Sun have made their way over to stand behind her. Shaven-headed freaks.

I give them a look of regal contempt and depart from their presence. I intend to find a little peace. Magdalen and some other Shaolin Queens beckon me over to their table. I avoid them and head for a quiet corner, but there are no quiet corners. I'll settle for anywhere I can think. Loretta Dragon Slayer appears alongside me and tells me to name my price for the *Venus de Milo*, because John the Brute is getting impatient.

'Do you mean he's actually going to pay me for it?'

Loretta Dragon Slayer puts her face next to mine.

'Are you suggesting that my employer is dishonest?'

'Well, he does call himself the Bandit King of the Red Mountains,' I point out. 'Hardly a name to give confidence to anyone wishing to sell him something.'

Loretta now has an expression on her face you might have thought she'd reserve for a dragon she particularly disliked.

'Just name your price, Trader.'

'1,000,000 zoobies.'

'What's the matter?' she asks. 'Are you tired of living?'

I depart swiftly. Unable to find a corner of Big Mary's Bar and Grill that is not positively overflowing with Dragon Slayers, bookmakers, Shaolin Queens, Ninjas and suchlike, all of them after me for something, I head for the door. Outside it's cold and wet, but at least there won't be anyone wishing to harm me.

It is day thirty-eight of the rains, and the area outside Big Mary's Bar and Grill is now a freezing swamp on to which more water is falling all the time. Big Mary's place is slightly raised, with huge drains running underneath. These cope with most of the excess, but, even so, water is beginning to trickle under the door. We are on a sloping plain here and not prone to floods, which is just as well. I don't want to find myself floating on a raft with Tank Girl and John the Brute. What a terrible thought!

I let the rain soak into my skin. It's uncomfortable out here in the wind and the rain, but my head is clearing. Looking over at the new supercharged Big Trader Truck with its XTF 98 engine, I feel reassured. If flight becomes inevitable there is no way anyone will catch me.

I can't think what to do about the *Venus de Milo*, but in the meantime it is most important for me not to be knocked out of the card-game. I will have to cheat. That is risky, though. Rumours are circulating that I cheated already. Curse that Magdalen and her big-mouthed sisters. They can't prove a thing. They're watching me, though.

I gaze off into the distance, where there is nothing to see whatsoever except rain. When the rain stops, the desert will bloom. Very pretty it is too, and we have a reasonable climate for about four days before everything starts drying out and the place reverts to its usual hot, arid and uncomfortable state. I wonder if there are any more pleasant continents anywhere. Maybe I could go and start a new life somewhere else. I'm just musing on this when three assassins roll up in an amphibious truck carrying heavy armaments, get out and push their way roughly past me into the Bar and Grill. The doorman shouts after them that they've forgotten to check in their guns. Good joke.

Well, this is a surprise. No one usually hires assassins during the rainy season. I know they are assassins, of course, because they are wearing black bandannas wrapped round their heads and they all have 'Hit Man' tattooed on their brawny arms. Who have they come for? I wonder. I hope it's ZugZug. Maybe she has outraged some rich citizen by giving him bad odds on a bet.

Firing erupts inside the Bar and Grill, followed by shouting, screaming and the sounds of bodies flying around. I am tempted to take a look inside, but wisely decide against it. You never know who might get shot when the assassins come in.

After a while the firing dies down. I decide to risk a look inside because I am freezing to death out here. Before I reach the door, it flies open, and a very annoyed-looking Tank Girl drags out the bodies of two of the assassins. Behind her Jet Girl is hauling out the other one.

'Well, I mean, I'm furious,' says Tank Girl. 'Absolutely livid. I can't ever remember being so insulted. I mean, *three* assassins? *Three*? The last person who wanted to kill me sent twenty. What's the idea of publicly implying that three assassins might be enough to defeat me? This sort of thing could ruin my reputation. I tell you, I'm furious.'

They go back into Big Mary's Bar and Grill, leaving the dead assassins to sink down in the mud. I stare at their bodies. Tank Girl is right, of course. Setting three assassins on to her is nothing short of stupid. Whoever wanted to kill her must be a very cheap sort of person not to have hired more.

23

Steam rises off me as the fierce heat in Big Mary's dries my clothes. The excitement caused by the assassination attempt seems to have died down already. Tank Girl dealing with three hired killer-assassins is not that unusual a sight for anybody around here. Nothing they won't have seen before. There is not even much speculation about who might have sent them, and, in fact, I never actually learn who it was. Assassins are after Tank Girl all the time. Even she loses track of who is out to get her. Whenever the assassins come, she just routinely dispatches them and gets on with whatever she was doing at the time.

With only enough money left for one game, I try and raise a little money from Alvin. He is keen to buy the fuzzbox, but claims that he will only be able to afford 100 zoobies, and not even that till the end of the night, when Big Mary pays him for the gig.

'Fine, Alvin. If ZugZug gets me you can pay it to my immediate family, wherever they might be.'

Tank Girl bangs her fist on the table and proclaims that it is now time for the game to recommence. I fondly wish that someone would bang her head on the table. Everyone makes their way wearily over. Iris Grim interrupts my still rather unsteady progress.

'I'll give you 600 for the statue,' she says.

Word of its value must be getting around.

I tell her that the Shaolin Queens have already offered me double that. She tells me that she knows I am lying.

Thirty-eight hours' drinking must have dulled my negotiating skills.

I sit down and put in my stake, the last of my money. Booga has not made it back to the table, so his pile of money goes into the pot.

'Well, well. The Trader's down to his last zoobie,' says Tank Girl. 'Better not break his concentration. Everyone be quiet while the Trader tries desperately to stay in the game. No one speak in case it puts the Trader off, and he is obliged to pay ZugZug 500 zoobies he doesn't have. Do not under any circumstances remind the Trader what a good shot ZugZug is, and what a short temper she has. Try not to bring it to the Trader's attention that ZugZug and four of her cronies are standing right behind him at this moment. Don't mention it at all. Just let him play out his final hand to the best of his ability. Remember, it's the playing that counts, not the winning. If the Trader gets booted out the game after losing this hand, he'll still have done well to get so far. On no account tell the Trader that, while he was out of the room, there were no takers for bets on his life expectancy. Anyone who says this may well distract him from his game, and that is the last thing we want. Are you ready to play, Trader? Just give it your best shot. No one can expect any more than that. Not putting you off, am I?'

I glower at her. She smiles sweetly back at me. The Professor shuffles the cards.

'Where was I in my story?' continues Tank Girl. 'Just about to carry out the final raid on Water and Power if I remember correctly, and to rescue Sam from the pipe. Did I mention that Kesslee had put Sam in the pipe, where she was in severe danger of drowning? I only discovered this later, of course. Kesslee was keen on putting people in that pipe. Not sure why. Odd habit though, but there again, so's stamp-collecting. In fact, stamp-collecting might be even odder than putting people in pipes.'

'Train-spotting is really odd,' Jet Girl comments.

'Yes, quite bizarre,' agrees Tank Girl. 'Especially as there aren't any trains any more. Doesn't stop them, though. Did Kesslee actually collect pipes, or did he just have one particular favourite? I never got round to asking.'

The Professor deals, and I try to concentrate on the cards.

'Immediately we started considering how to carry out the attack, I came up with an extra-good idea, which was to paint Jet Girl's jet so it looked like a proper military aircraft jet again, as Jet Girl had recently painted it pink. So, we headed over to the desert workshop where Sub Girl used to hang around, looking for a paint job.'

'Sub Girl used to hang around in a workshop?' says the Professor, quizzically.

'What's wrong with that?'

'Well, if Water and Power were so all-powerful that they controlled the whole continent, how is it that Sub Girl could run an illegal workshop big enough to paint a jet fighter in? Didn't they notice?'

'What an irritating person you are,' says Tank Girl. 'Stop raising ridiculous objections to my story. If I say Sub Girl had a big workshop, then she had a big workshop. She used to disguise it as a coffee and croissant shop during the day.

'Sub Girl was there as usual, building her submarine,

or so she claimed, and going on about the rains coming and get your umbrellas mended and make ready for the deluge. We flew the jet in and gave it a paint job.'

Tank Girl glances over to see if the Professor has any more objections to make, but the Professor hasn't. He has nodded gently off to sleep. The extended card-playing and drinking have proved too much for him. He misses his turn and is out of the game. I am still concentrating fiercely and do not even look up as the Professor's money is pushed into the middle of the table. Along with Booga's cash, this makes it a very valuable game. The only players now remaining are myself, Tank Girl, Jet Girl, Sub Girl and Donner.

Tank Girl, well aware of this, redoubles her efforts to put everyone off and starts waving her arms about again and perching on the card-table, pretending she's sitting in her tank leading the troops forward. She describes sending Jet Girl and the Rippers off in the jet to carry out a frontal assault while she carried out a cunning pincer movement with her tank.

'I raced over miles of trackless desert, travelling by night and sleeping by day. Not a beer passed my lips as I grimly made my way forward. As a strategic advance, it was magnificent. Napoleonic, even. And then, after I avoided the outposts that guarded the approaches, do you know what I did?'

'What did you do, Tank Girl?' asks Donner.

'You want to know what I did?'

'Tell us, Tank Girl –'

'*Snap!*' I say, being wise to this tactic, and fling my entire body on top of the last card played.

'It's mine, it's mine!' I scream. 'I won, I'm still in the game!'

114

This would be true were it not for the fact that I have called wrongly and thrown my entire body over a queen played on a king, not on another queen, as I had thought.

'The Trader goes to pieces,' roars Tank Girl with a huge grin, and she seems quite amused by my desperation.

Dignity in shreds, I retake my chair. Play continues; Tank Girl continues.

'What I did was to get in my trusty paraglider and make a silent aerial approach. Brilliant, though I say it myself. If the guards were expecting me, this was bound to surprise them. "Where is Tank Girl?" they'd say, scanning the desert for signs of a tank. "We can't see her anywhere." Meanwhile, I was up above them, floating into a perfect landing, guns, grenades and catapult poised to start dealing mayhem and taking out the enemy.

'Meanwhile, Jet Girl and the kangaroos were approaching the base from the other side. Jet Girl, previously a shy, softly spoken introvert, had now changed entirely under the benign influence of the Tank Girl "Beer and Barfing" assertiveness course. This involves drinking so much you don't give a shit what anyone thinks, and I've always found it works very well. So, while the kangaroos were arguing with her, and T-Saint was trying to take control of the mission, Jet Girl now had no difficulty in slapping him down and getting the troops in order and ready to land.

'Using security codes that Jet Girl had secretly learned while working at the base as a mechanic, they landed without causing suspicion. Everyone thought it was a proper Water and Power jet and they taxied into a hangar. Now was the moment. We were all in position. I'd programmed my tank to come smashing through the outer fences, drawing the defenders' fire while the rest of us sneaked up on them from behind.

'So there we were, all set to go.

'"Let's boogie," I said. And my tank came crashing into the base. Battle had begun.'

Tank Girl, not pausing for breath, or apparently paying any attention, suddenly slams her hand down on to the pile of cards. She's won the round. Unless I can raise some money in the next thirty seconds I am out of the game.

24

At this crucial moment in history, when I am facing complete defeat, and Tank Girl is in the ascendant, Jet Girl begins to act very strangely. It's her turn to deal but she just sits there grinning stupidly for a while before starting to giggle. Her giggle swells quickly into a manic laugh. She thrusts her chair back, leaps to her feet and makes funny faces at Donner.

Oh dear. Poor Jet Girl. It's obvious she's about to lose it completely. Up to now she has been seen sitting quietly at the table, commenting occasionally on Tank Girl's story, drinking her beer and playing cards. For the past hour or so she has been exhibiting signs of tiredness, but, instead of drifting off to sleep from the effects of drink, she is now gripped by a fit of dementia. It's as if forty hours' alcohol have built up inside her to suddenly burst through in a tidal wave of crazed behaviour.

She leaps on to the table, sticks out her arms like wings and starts going 'Whee!' 'Vroom! Vroom!' and making other similar noises, and pretending she's flying her jet. Everyone's cards and money are trodden underfoot as the demented pilot starts picking up glasses and throwing them about shouting 'bombs away', and 'take that, you swine', and a lot more stuff that I don't quite catch.

I am appalled at this unwarranted disruption of the card-game, but Tank Girl, being uncivilized and a boor, just throws back her head and screams with laughter.

So amused is she at her friend's insane behaviour, that she leaps on to the table with her and starts pretending to be a tank. A few seconds later the pair of maniacs are pounding round on the table causing mayhem and destruction, the Shaolin Queens and others sitting around are falling about laughing and Big Mary is stomping her way over to see what all the fuss is about. Meanwhile, Donner is showing some concern, but Sub Girl just sits with a sneer on her face. She withdraws slightly from the table to avoid the flying feet and glasses.

'Enemy target ahead,' yells Jet Girl. 'Launch the smart bomb.' She throws a pint of lager into the crowd.

'Suck on these, scumbags!' shouts Tank Girl, raining peanuts over everyone.

Jet Girl starts to fall. Donner leaps up on to the table to support her. Unfortunately, the table is not strong enough to support two women and a kangaroo and it collapses in a heap, mainly on top of me. Outraged, I claw my way free of the carnage and human destruction, as does Tank Girl. Neither Donner nor Jet Girl gets up from the floor. The fall and the alcohol have done for them both, and they lie in a messy pile with Little Wee Sam on the ground.

Tank Girl thinks it is all a huge joke and cackles with laughter. I am not pleased.

'I shall send a strong complaint about these diversionary tactics to the organizing committee!' I say. 'I demand you award me the prize now.'

No one pays any attention. They are all too busy gathering up their money from the floor before any of the thousands of thieves and criminals in Big Mary's can get their hands on it.

'Way to go, Jet Girl!' screams Tank Girl, as Big Mary and a few others haul her friend and the kangaroo to a corner to sleep it off.

Despite my outrage I feel sorry for Jet Girl, dragged away drunk and unconscious after her bout of extremely disorderly behaviour. I expect she was a quiet and genteel young woman before falling under the malign influence of Tank Girl. No doubt she will regret it in the morning.

Big Mary is also displeased and informs us gruffly that she will expect to be paid for the broken table out of the winnings. One might have thought that with all the money the card-game has brought into the bar, Big Mary could stand the loss of a cheap old table, but she is a mean woman, hardened against any acts of kindness and understanding by years of running a bar in the Wastelands, where every second person is a total maniac and a hazard to your health. And, of course, she's had Tank Girl to cope with for forty-one hours, which would be enough to get anyone down.

Various members of the bar-staff cluster around trying to repair things and it is necessary for us players to take an unscheduled break. This miraculous disruption in the proceedings gives me a chance. While any player running out of money during the game is deemed to be out of the competition, an exception is made if his or her running out of money coincides with a break. You are allowed to try and raise money during a break. If I can rustle up a stake before the next hand starts, I'll be back in the game. An excellent stroke of luck, I think to myself, and hurry off to find Iris Grim.

The transaction does not take long. Iris Grim, imagining, I suppose, that she is party to valuable secret information about the statue, pays me the 600 zoobies quickly enough. She nods when I tell her not to take the statue till after the game.

'Don't even look at it. John the Brute is after it. There'll be trouble if he sees it and learns you've bought it.'

I rush back to the table. Tank Girl starts to commiserate with me for being out of the game, but I slap my new pile of money down triumphantly.

'I'm still here.'

She grins.

'Well, well. How did you raise that? Something immoral which you'll soon regret, I don't doubt. So you're still in, Trader. Just you, me and Sub Girl left.'

She slaps me on the back before striding off to the bar screaming for more beer and a pizza.

'And a bowl of cornflakes with a banana on top,' she adds. 'And slice the banana up evenly, but don't let any of the slices drop into the milk. And put the sugar on the cornflakes before you put the banana slices on.'

Ootsie, vainly imagining that Sub Girl might need comforting after the furore at the card-table, actually tries to put his young hand on her leather-clad shoulder.

She gives him a look that says something like, 'move that hand before I chop it off and ram it down your throat,' and he removes it hurriedly. Poor Ootsie. You can't comfort a hardened thug like Sub Girl. The sort of person who goes on incredible drinking binges with Tank Girl, then sails around in a huge submarine shooting torpedoes at things, tormenting the fish and creating havoc across the seven seas, is not the sort of person who is going to quietly hold hands in a bar. Ootsie has just picked the wrong woman and should settle for a nice shop-assistant in Lugit City, if he could find one who wasn't too put off by his strange and arcane Ninja practices. But he remains sitting behind Sub Girl anyway, looking at her with quiet adoration. Idiot.

It's funny how inspiration can strike at the strangest times. Anyone contemplating my desperate situation – surrounded by enemies on all sides, the *Venus de Milo* sold to three separate people, each of whom is going to be upset about it at the end, John the Brute and ZugZug breathing down my neck, Tank Girl and Sub Girl both being much more sober than me – might expect that I would be hard pushed just to keep going, never mind come up with cunning plans. But that's the way I am. Put the Trader in a tight spot, and he'll come up with something exceptional. The grimmer the situation, the more resolute the Trader becomes. Ask anyone in the Wastelands, they'll tell you.

So, it is at this star-crossed moment that I realize why I have been doing so badly in the drinking competition and card-game: Tank Girl and Sub Girl are much better drinkers and card-players than me. Fine. See if I care. I know what to do about it.

I lurch over to the bar and seek out Grid the Barman, who I am very friendly with, due to my letting him in on some favourable deals. I have always found it pays to keep in with barmen.

'Grid. Does Big Mary still sell that terrible palm-tree vodka, the stuff that's unbelievably potent and tastes of nothing at all?'

He nods.

'Well, start spiking the beer that's being served to Tank Girl and Sub Girl. A few shots of that in their lager and they'll be lucky to keep breathing, never mind playing cards.'

Grid is dubious.

'Why should I do that?' he asks.

'Because we're friends.'

'I might lose my job.'

'I'll give you a hefty bribe.'

We negotiate, and I am a little disappointed that Grid demands such a high price, seeing as we're friends and everything, but eventually we come to an agreement. I'm chuckling as I head back to the game. Tank Girl and Sub Girl won't know what's hit them.

Loretta Dragon Slayer interrupts me again.

'Nice samurai outfit,' I tell her, being sociable.

She ignores the compliment. I don't know why I bother.

'The statue. John the Brute is getting impatient.'

I explain that there are only three of us left in the game, and I have every reason to believe that it will soon be over. Surely even John the Brute would not wrench a man away from the Annual Wastelands Snap and Drinking Competition only moments before his ultimate triumph?

'And afterwards he can have the *Venus de Milo* for only 100,000 zoobies. A bargain.'

Our attention is diverted by a pathetic wailing noise. This wailing noise is emanating from Bitsy, who is in a sorry state. Tank Girl has emptied a bowl of cornflakes and bananas over his head. Mingling with his blue hair, it makes for a very sad sight.

'Tank Girl is terrible,' he wails. I paid her a compliment and she emptied a bowl of cornflakes and bananas over my head. I hate her.'

He wanders off, wreathed in misery. Very sad. But all for the best, really. Having fallen in love with Tank Girl, he was probably lucky to escape with only a bowl of cornflakes over his head. Others have suffered far worse.

25

There are now only three of us left in the game.

'Tension mounts,' declares Tank Girl as we take our seats. She's a terrible woman for speaking in clichés.

'You've done well to come this far, Sub Girl, ol' buddy. Wouldn't have thought you had it in you. People might say you're a bit of a freak, hanging around in that submarine most of the time playing with the sharks, but I've always liked you. Even back in the days when you just used to bore everyone to death with your prophecies, I liked you. Under my tuition you've come on well. Don't worry what people say about you behind your back, I believe in you. You'll entirely deserve second place in the competition.'

Sub Girl does not react to this at all. She sits at the table, cold as a fish. Maybe this is why she spends so much time underwater. Yes, I may have hit on something there.

'As for you, Trader,' continues Tank Girl. 'You are a cheating, thieving, lying cur. I hope ZugZug cuts you up into little bits. But hey, nothing personal.'

'What makes you think you're going to win, Tank Girl?'

She grins her huge grin.

'I always win. I'm the undefeated champion of everything.'

Not this time, I think to myself grimly, as Grid the Barman brings up the spiked drinks. Tank Girl, whose greed matches her ego, guzzles down half her pint and starts to ramble on again.

'So, we'd busted into the base. The attack force was all in position, that is, me, Jet Girl and the Rippers. But this was only the first part, things weren't over by a long way. Remember it was just the eight of us against the huge, well-equipped and highly disciplined army of Water and Power, complete with their astonishing array of tanks, big guns, small guns, fighter planes, bombers, attack helicopters, assault craft and lots of other neat stuff.' She pauses.

'I've always liked advanced weaponry. Don't know why, just a natural affinity, I suppose. It's mutual, though. My tank loves me.'

She waves out the window to her tank. As far as I can see it doesn't wave back. Maybe it's just tired.

'And beer, of course. I've always had a natural affinity to beer.'

She sips the rest of her drink. Knowing that it is now laced with Big Mary's lethal palm-tree vodka, I have to make an effort not to laugh. Take that, Tank Girl. Not even you will be able to down many pints of that stuff. Play resumes, as Tank Girl, losing the thread of her story, mutters on about beer and tanks.

At some time during the evening Tank Girl has applied some face paint in two lines under each eye, rather like the warpaint worn by the Post-Apocalypse Biker Girls, though black rather than green, and less extensive. It looks ridiculous to me, but she is obviously well pleased with the effect, as she keeps pointing it out to those around her like a small child with a new dress. However, as she is unable to leave it alone and keeps fingering her face, the lines are now slightly smudged. In the heat a few tiny rivulets of paint are starting to flow very slowly down her cheeks.

I notice Iris Grim edging her way towards the *Venus de Milo*, which is still sitting in the dark corner on a chair wearing the combat jacket and the baseball cap. I am anxious in case Iris does anything too obvious, like shouting 'the *Venus de Milo*! It's worth 1,000,000 zoobies and it's all mine!', which would really upset all the other people I've sold it to, and totally infuriate John the Brute, but she doesn't. She just looks at it, nodding her head-dress slightly. Iris Grim, like all the Post-Apocalypse Biker Girls, is still wearing her green buzzard feather head-dress and warpaint. Brightens the place up, I suppose. It makes for an unusual sight when they're riding their motorbikes over the sand-dunes.

Bitsy, I notice, is finding Iris Grim interesting. He is standing close to her with a familiar dumb look on his face.

While I am studying Iris Grim's head-dress, Sub Girl wins the hand. I wrench my attention back to the game. My pile of money is by far the smallest of the three, and I have to win regularly to stay in. ZugZug is, meanwhile, perched behind me like a vulture, along with two Children of the Temple of the Sun.

'Stop that bloody chanting,' I snarl. They ignore me.

Tank Girl gets back into action.

'Yes siree, we still had a lot of work to do. A whole army to defeat, in fact. The plan was for Jet Girl and the kangaroos to take care of the army while I went after Kesslee and rescued Sam. When my tank burst in through the perimeter fence, blasting everything in sight, I set off for Kesslee's office, hoping to take him by surprise. Most of the soldiers were running down to the tank to see what all the noise was, but they left a few guards behind them. I despatched them in my usual efficient way, cracking a few jokes to keep the atmosphere light, and pounded into the administration block.

'Things became a bit difficult here, however. I got lost. Remember, almost every time I'd been here before I'd been in manacles and chains and was shot full of bubonic plague or yellow fever or some other damn thing, so it was only natural that I should become a little disorientated. After crashing round the canteen, the executive toilets and the indoor putting range – quite difficult this, it took me five putts on the eighteenth – I found myself in the treasure-room, that fabulous Eldoradon vault rumoured to be full of all the art treasures looted from the world by Water and Power.

'I blasted a few old Italian paintings and Greek vases for target practice before I realized that, really, I shouldn't destroy them all, because, after I'd defeated Kesslee, the stuff would become mine by right of conquest and I could probably swap the *Mona Lisa* for quite a few beers. So I just patted a statue on the head and blasted my way out through –'

She pauses, and shakes her head.

'I just patted a statue on the head and blasted –'

She pauses again. Some dim thought appears to be taking shape inside her head. She swivels in her chair and looks directly at the *Venus de Milo*. She stares at it for a while.

'I just patted a statue on the head,' she says, more slowly, 'and blasted my way through the back wall. Leaving the art treasures behind. The art treasures which were going to be mine by right of conquest after the battle. The art treasures which included a particularly valuable statue.'

She stares at me. A rather penetrating stare, I must admit.

'Trader, have you been excavating on the ruins of Water and Power headquarters?'

I shake my head.

'Not me. Don't even know where it is. And it's all covered in sand these days. So I'm told, anyway. By people who've been there. I've never even seen it. My deal, is it?'

I grab the cards and deal them out quickly. Tank Girl gives the impression that she may have more to say on this matter, but lets it go for the moment.

'Eventually, I found Kesslee's office, but he wasn't there, so I wrecked it for fun. Incinerated his executive toys, scribbled over his wall-charts and spat in the fish-tanks. Outside I could hear the battle warming up as Jet Girl and the Rippers took on the army. I would pause here and step aside to let Jet Girl describe the scene, but, as Jet Girl is unfortunately unconscious in the far corner, I'll just have to describe it myself the best I can.'

At this moment I triumphantly win a round; my first success for a long time. My spirits are lifted. Perhaps the palm-tree vodka is slowing them down already.

'Drink up,' I say cheerily, and rake in my winnings.

26

As Sub Girl shuffles the cards, my concentration is interrupted by Loretta Dragon Slayer hissing in my ear, practically rupturing my eardrum, 'John the Brute is getting impatient.'

'I can't stop now,' I hiss back. 'Be reasonable. I'm close to winning. Alvin will be back onstage soon, tell John to go down the front and dance.'

'Are you trying to be funny, Trader? John the Brute does not dance.'

'Well, he should. It's fine exercise. Encourage him, he's probably just shy. Or take him for a walk in the rain. Entertain him with stories about all the dragons you've slain. I can't do business when I'm at the card-table. Tell him –'

A cunning thought strikes me.

'– tell him that Tank Girl absolutely refuses to let me away from the card-table until the game is finished. Were it not for her I'd be over there doing business with John the Brute right at this moment.'

Nothing like sowing a little discord between your enemies, and putting the blame on someone else.

'Suddenly, Sam's voice came over the tannoy system,' bawls Tank Girl, cranking herself up again. 'Fortu-nately, just audible over the sound of battle. "Help me, help me! Kesslee's put me upside down in a pipe full of water, and it's reached my nose. I'm going to drown!"

'I raced all over the damn place looking for that pipe, all the time giving battle to the soldiers and tanks that were streaming in from all directions. They came at me in waves, it was incredible. I had a machine-gun in my left hand and a baseball bat in my right and I just mowed them down in droves.

'"Oh no, it's Tank Girl!" they screamed. "We can't deal with this at all. Send for reinforcements."

'What with all the explosions, and smoke and fire everywhere, it was becoming hard to see anything, and I might never have found the pipe containing Little Wee Sam had I not at that moment practically tripped over Kesslee, who was standing by a wall, all square-jawed and with a steely glint in his eye. He was wearing his new cyber-arm, complete with whirring blades and jagged saws. A terrifying weapon. Must have made it impossibly difficult going for a wee, I would have thought. Maybe he paid an assistant to help him.

'"Your time has come, burger-brain," I yelled, and lunged at him with the baseball bat. I gave him a blow that would have torn him in half had he not turned out to be merely a hologram. My baseball bat went right through it, leaving me somewhat confused. Another Kesslee appeared behind me. The real one or another hologram? One way to find out: I mashed its head with the baseball bat. It was another hologram.

'"Kesslee, you cowardly scumbag, come out and fight," I yelled, becoming frustrated. I'd gone there to kill Kesslee, overthrow Water and Power and usher in a whole new world order, not dance around in a light-show. Another Kesslee appeared on a balcony. I leapt up and prepared to pulverize him, but he flickered and disappeared, leaving me on my own, once more frustrated and unfulfilled. And then, yet another Kesslee appeared below, looking up at the balcony.

'"Ah, Juliet," he said. Why he said that I have no idea. Just forgot my name, I suppose.

'"Kesslee," I roared. "You have the brains and the courage of a plankton. Stop mucking around with these holograms and come out and fight."

'"Why should I fight?" he asked. "I've already won. You see, Tank Girl, I've been playing with you all along."

'"No one plays with Tank Girl," I shouted back. "Apart from myself, of course."

'"I've been planning this for a long time," he said, quite coolly, considering there was a major battle going on around him. "I knew you were coming. You see, I've been listening to your every word for the past two months. When you were last here we planted a listening device in the freckles on your arm."

'Well,' says Tank Girl, looking round the table. 'I have to admit, this made me pause. What's the world coming to if you can't call your freckles your own? I mean, I must have had loads of conversations in the past two months I wouldn't have wanted Kesslee to hear. Or any stranger. You know the sort of thing – important battle plans, strategic discussions, attempts to borrow money from Booga for a can of beer. And then there was my sex-life. I'm not a woman who keeps quiet in bed, you know. Neighbours complain frequently, but I believe in saying what I want. I really hated the thought of Kesslee and his minions listening to all that.

'"You mean you engineered all this just so you could listen to me shagging?"

'"No, Tank Girl. I have little interest in your shagging. I engineered all this so you would bring me the

Rippers. Save me the trouble of going and finding them. You've walked into a trap. Once we wipe you and the Rippers out, the Blue Dunes will be mine. I will control the entire continent, thanks to you."

'"Help me! Help me! The water's rising," came Sam's voice over the tannoy.

'"Oh dear," said Kesslee. "Looks like Sam isn't going to make it."'

Tank Girl slams her fist on the table where play is going round quickly between the three of us.

'I was now completely infuriated. I mean *really* angry. If there's one thing that really bugs me, it's being manipulated by powerful forces beyond my control. Who did this freak think he was, putting listening devices in my freckles and shoving my young friend down a pipe? Not reasonable behaviour at all. Now, I am often criticized for being violent, but surely no one could object if I ripped this man limb from limb. Which is what I now set out to do.

'I leapt over the balcony and proceeded to give him hell with the baseball bat. To my relief, this was actually the real Kesslee – I had had quite enough of the holo-grams – but the fight didn't prove quite as easy as I thought. His cyber-arm had been well constructed, and every time I took a swing at him he'd block it with one of the blades, cutting a piece off my bat till eventually I was facing him with only a small stump of wood in my hand. I had, unfortunately, left the machine-gun on the balcony.

'Kesslee laughed and said he'd been looking forward to this for some time. He revved up the arm to full power, quoted a few duff lines from a poem and ran right at me. We had an intense duel, during which he attempted to cut me into little pieces with his cyber-arm, and I attempted to knock his head off with any-thing that came to hand. Back and forwards we fought, along the corridors and up and down the stairs, while all around us chaos reigned. The Rippers were fighting it out with the soldiers, and bullets and plasma-beams were flying around in all directions.

'Kesslee was a mean fighter, but I gave him a few good whacks and was definitely ahead on points when misfortune struck. I slipped on something – potato peelings from the canteen, I think, though I couldn't absolutely swear to it – and tumbled down at Kesslee's feet, bumping my head rather painfully in the process.

'"Ow!" I said. Kesslee kicked me while I was down, and I rolled on to this walkway that ran between two buildings. It was held in place by these steel cables, and Kesslee cut right through one of them with his cyber-arm. The walkway started to sway around, and there I was, hanging on grimly to this swaying lump of metal, while Kesslee took aim at the other cable. When he cut it, I was going to plummet to my doom. Only seconds to live. A bad situation. I can't deny it. And then –'

Everyone's attention is on Tank Girl.

'*Snap!*' she says, winning the hand.

I am furious. Completely disgruntled. I should know better by now.

I drink down my beer. This is a very difficult task, requiring a Herculean effort. The beer actually seems to be fighting back. I have drunk more beer in the past forty-three hours than is humanly possible. I must have a tankerful inside me. Sub Girl drinks hers and, for the first time, she looks a little queasy. I'm thinking that I really cannot go on for much longer when Big Mary, still heavily armed, marches up and announces another break.

Sub Girl rises slowly and leaves the table with an unsteady tread. I rise even more slowly and try to remember where I am, what I'm doing and where the toilet is. Tank Girl claps Magdalen on the shoulder and asks her to buy her a beer, as she seems to have finished hers already, and is feeling a little thirsty.

27

I'm sitting on the floor in Big Mary's Bar and Grill. Where exactly on the floor, I'm not sure. My endurance has come to an end. The game is due to restart any moment, but I know I will be unable to rise again. I'm beaten.

'The Trader is never beaten,' I tell myself, and make a determined effort to get up on to my feet. Nothing happens. I can't move.

'The Trader is beaten,' I tell myself, and abandon all hope.

Ootsie comes and sits down beside me. Great. Just what I need. The lovelorn Ninja has come to torment me with his idiocy.

'Trader, I can't stand it. I'm so in love with Sub Girl, and she refuses to even acknowledge my existence.'

I admire her willpower.

'Give up, Ootsie. It's hopeless.'

'Why?'

'Because you're a nice young guy, and she's a pain in the neck without any human emotions whatsoever.'

Ootsie looks hurt. Unfortunately, he does not go away. He denies that Sub Girl is lacking in emotions.

'They're just buried deep. I'm sure if we went away together for a holiday in her submarine I could awaken them.'

He wants to go away in her submarine for a holiday. I shake my head.

'Ootsie. Do you notice anything about me? Like, for

instance, I am sitting here completely unable to move when I should be back at the card-table? I am in a bad state, and when ZugZug gets hold of me it's going to get worse. Why, in these circumstances, are you boring me with your stupid emotional problems?'

'I've no one else to talk to,' says Ootsie, sadly. 'You must help me, Trader. Eldrich San is planning to take us all on a training exercise to the far side of the continent, and Sub Girl will sail away in her submarine, and I might never see her again. I'm desperate.'

I try and think of some way to get Ootsie to leave me alone to my misery.

'Buy her a nice present,' I suggest.

He seems to like this idea.

'A nice present! Of course! The very thing! What will I get her?'

I consider this for a few moments.

'How about a statue of a mermaid? Bound to go down well with her. She'd be so grateful she'd fall into your arms.'

'Where would I get a statue of a mermaid?'

'Well, by a tremendous coincidence, Ootsie, I happen to have one with me. And it's yours for only 100 zoobies.'

'I'll take it!' he cries.

The Trader does it again. There are no circumstances in which I will not do profitable business.

Ootsie hurries away to get the money. How he will raise 100 zoobies, I can't imagine, but the power of love is a remarkable thing, and not long after he comes back with a little purse of money. Now, nothing revives my spirits like a profitable sale and I feel a slight surge of energy.

'The statue is yours. Now, help me back to the table and I promise to put in a good word for you.'

Ootsie practically has to carry me back in his arms. He sits me down in my chair and I try to focus my eyes on the table. Tank Girl is hugely amused by all this and mocks me at length, but I notice, dimly, that Sub Girl is not doing all that much better. She is swaying in her chair and has extreme difficulty shuffling the cards. They spill out of her hands, and there is a sequence of pantomime as she tries to pick them up off the floor. Eventually, the attentive Ootsie does it for her, and she slowly starts to deal.

'Looks like it's game to me,' announces Tank Girl. She drinks down some palm-tree-vodka-enhanced beer and reaches for another. I'm amazed. The woman is simply inhuman. Is there no limit at all to her capacity? I foresee health problems for her in the future.

28

Unexpectedly, we are joined at the table by Jet Girl. Having passed out some time ago after the now notorious 'dancing on the table' incident, she is out of the game, but, having now woken up, has come to see what's happening. I am impressed by her stamina. I know that when I finally pass out, I will be gone for a week at least. Mining Jim, Wanda the Gun Dealer, the Professor, the kangaroos and sundry other players who fell by the wayside earlier are all still slumped in corners and under tables.

The card-table is now surrounded by a great host of people, all jostling for position to see the final outcome of the game. Wasteland Ninjas rub up against Post-Apocalypse Biker Boys, who peer over the shoulders of Shaolin Queens and Post-Apocalypse Biker Girls. Miners, traders, vagrants, nomads, drinkers, gamblers and musicians all struggle for space, all talking loudly about the game, while placing bets with ZugZug and her helpers. Even the Four Dwarfs can be seen shouldering their way through the crowd to have a look. On-stage, members of Alvin's band perch on their amplifiers to see over the crowd.

The colours of the gangs, the mirror fragments and red topknots of the Shaolin Queens, the Biker Girls' green-feathered head-dresses and warpaint, the Biker Boys' shredded denim and yellow bandannas, the Ninjas' blue hair and black cloaks and the Children of the Temple of the Sun's orange robes all touch, and clash to create the brightest assemblage of people ever seen in Big Mary's bar. The colours stand out garishly in the smoke-filled atmosphere through which the white-clad Big Mary and her barmen emerge occasionally carrying trays of beer and shouting out orders. Almost everybody seems to be drunk or stoned. Everyone is enjoying the occasion, and even the fierce rivalries of the gangs seem to be forgotten for a while as the game nears its climax.

The austere Loretta Dragon Slayer is not to be seen. No doubt she disapproves of frivolity. As for John the Brute, Bandit King of the Red Mountains, I last saw him staring into a bottle of rum on the far side of the bar. He would not want to see Tank Girl triumph, as most people watching now expect she will. There are few bets now being placed on Sub Girl, and fewer on me.

'Did I make a fool of myself?' Jet Girl asks, rather anxiously.

'Absolutely,' replies Tank Girl. 'A total fool. Possibly a new world record. People will never stop talking about it. "There's goes Jet Girl," they'll say, "the one who lost control and made a complete idiot of herself at the card-game."'

Jet Girl looks glum at the prospect.

'It might be forgotten in time,' adds Tank Girl brightly. 'But, fortunately, we've got it on video. Hey, Sub Girl! Deal the cards, will you? I'm getting bored waiting.'

Sub Girl is still having difficulty getting the cards under control. Tank Girl taps her fingers on the table impatiently.

'Jet Girl, why don't you tell us what was going on

with you and the Rippers when we invaded the Water and Power headquarters? Fill in a few details. Give them a rounded picture, you know. I don't want to give the impression I was the only hero that day. Of course, I was doing all the difficult stuff on my own, and there were nine of you, so I guess my part in the proceedings was the most impressive. Anyway, tell us what you were up to while I was fighting Kesslee.'

Jet Girl seems surprised, in a pleased sort of way.

'You actually want me to tell a story?'

'Sure,' says Tank Girl.

'You never usually let me get a word in.'

'Well, now's your chance, Jet Girl. The floor is yours.'

Jet Girl's long dark hair is matted around her face. She sweeps it back with her fingers and marshals her thoughts for a few seconds.

'After we landed in the hangar, everything was quiet. Too quiet, really –'

'What do you mean, "too quiet"?' demands Tank Girl. 'How could it be "too quiet"?'

'Well, I mean, it was a bit suspicious that it was so quiet.'

'Doesn't make much sense to me,' says Tank Girl. 'Either it was quiet, or it wasn't. I don't see how it could be too quiet. Too quiet for what?'

Jet Girl looks annoyed.

'Look, do you want me to tell this story or not?'

'Sure I do. Just get to the point, that's all.'

'I'm doing my best.'

I feel sorry for Jet Girl. It must be hell being friends with Tank Girl. She carries on with her tale.

'I told the Rippers to fan out and look out for trouble. It was dark in the hangar. We were going to get ourselves into position, ready for the attack, thinking we had the element of surprise –'

'What?' demands Tank Girl.

'The element of surprise.'

'What does that mean? What's an element of surprise?'

'You know what it means.'

'No, I don't.'

'It's a well-known expression.'

'Not to me, it isn't,' declares Tank Girl. 'I've never heard it before. You must have made it up. It doesn't mean anything. How can surprise have an element? How can surprise have anything? We're talking nonsense here, Jet Girl.'

Jet Girl looks around for some support, but none is forthcoming. I suppose, when you think about it closely, it is an odd expression. Still, I'm drunk, I can't really tell. For literary opinions you'd need to ask the Professor and he's still comatose.

Jet Girl starts to look upset.

'What's the matter with you, Tank Girl? You asked me to tell my story and now you keep interrupting.'

'Only because you keep coming out with meaningless rubbish. Just get to the point. No one wants to hear about the element of surprise being too quiet or any of that stuff. Complete balls, if you ask me. You're losing the attention of the public. Just tell the story like it happened.'

Jet Girl, however, now seems to be in a huff, and declines to speak any more.

'No wonder I never let you tell any stories,' says Tank Girl, whacking her palm down on to the table to emphasize the point. 'You get put off too easily. You start off and then refuse to finish. Well, I've heard it often enough from you, anyway. I'll tell it. Listen carefully and you'll get a few hints about how to tell a story properly.

'Subby, are you ever going to deal those cards? Get them out on the table or give up the game. Come on, I've been sat here for forty-four hours and my ass is starting to protest. It's high time this game was over and we were out of here. Deal 'em, Sub Girl.'

29

Sub Girl eventually manages to deal. I quickly win the hand, slamming a three of clubs down on a three of hearts with some enthusiasm. Grid the Barman pounds down the next round of beers, which Tank Girl and Sub Girl now have to drink. Seeing the difficulties Sub Girl is in, I can tell that the secret doses of palm-tree vodka are having a ruinous effect on her. There is, unfortunately, no sign of it working on Tank Girl, but it is bound to soon. I just have to hold on long enough.

Tank Girl, as always, empties her drink down her throat in one swift and greedy gulp before grabbing the cards to shuffle and deal, meanwhile taking up the story where Jet Girl gave up.

'So, there were Jet Girl and eight genetically enhanced kangaroos in a dark hangar, waiting for the attack to begin. As soon as my tank came smashing through the fence outside, they were ready to leap into action and start dealing out powerful blows to the enemy. They were only nine against an army, but you have to remember that the Rippers were pretty tough and also had this really neat body armour. Also, Jet Girl, for all her faults, is a good fighter.'

'Well, thank you,' says Jet Girl.

'You're welcome. Things started to go wrong immediately. Kesslee knew they were coming and his troops were lying in wait. While they were sneaking through the hangar, the lights suddenly went on, leaving them exposed in the middle. Soldiers appeared on the gantries all around and started laying into them with their rifles. Jet Girl and the kangaroos managed to flee behind some old oil-drums for a bit of temporary cover, but the situation was looking grim.

'"The lights, the lights!" they all screamed. "Someone put out the lights!" This is when the first recorded act of kangaroo heroism took place. Veetee, a brave, strong and worthy kangaroo, with selfless courage ran over the floor of the hangar and destroyed the fuse-box. Unfortunately, he was cut to pieces as he did so. Poor Veetee. He was only a humble kangaroo, and I never knew him all that well, and now I think about it I don't recall him ever actually buying me a drink or anything, but it was a valorous act and will be remembered whenever two or more kangaroos are gathered together to talk about old times. His name shall never be forgotten. Good old Veetee.'

'Actually, his name was Deetee,' says Jet Girl.

'No, it wasn't, it was Veetee.'

'Deetee.'

'Veetee.'

'I tell you it was Deetee,' insists Jet Girl.

Tank Girl shrugs.

'Well, Deetee then, if you must. Who the hell cares what his name was? The point is, it'll never be forgotten. Now, stop interrupting. I'm simply trying to explain that the rest of the kangaroos were furious about his death. They didn't stand around debating what his name was, they just shed a few brief, manly kangaroo tears, then proceeded to attack under cover of darkness and give the soldiers hell.

'It was an incredible battle. Squadrons of troops racing through the vast hangar with guns blazing, only to find that their target was no longer there but had bounced right over them and was attacking from behind. The Rippers, driven into a fury by the death of Veetee, fought like madmen, or mad kangaroos, I should say, and soon gained the upper hand. The soldiers retreated, leaving the mangled corpses of their companions where they lay.

' "Forward!" cried Jet Girl, and led them on out of the hangar towards the main concentration of troops in the barracks outside.'

Tank Girl stops. She looks around her with a slightly puzzled air, as if something odd has just come to her attention. She glares at her empty glass suspiciously, then picks it up and sniffs it.

'Funny beer,' she mutters, and glances around her curiously. As I am busy concentrating on my cards I do not meet her eyes.

She frowns and starts talking again.

All the while the game is going round faster and faster. Tank Girl is still winning, and I am still in the poorest position, but Sub Girl is starting to fade badly. She cannot win a hand, and the pile of money in front of her starts to shrink as she loses stake after stake.

'Jet Girl led the Rippers out of the hangar and into the base at the same moment my tank powered its way in. Caught between two enemies, the Water and Power troops panicked, particularly when they heard that the dreaded Tank Girl was among them, come to wreak her revenge on her former tormentors.'

Tank Girl, pleased with this phrase, repeats it.

'Yes sir, come to wreak her revenge on her former tormentors. And while I was busy wreaking my revenge, Jet and the Rippers were mowing down the soldiers like nobody's business. Fortunately, most of the heavy weaponry in the base was pointing out of the way, as they had never expected to be infiltrated in such a cunning manner. While they were trying to turn their guns round and put their tanks into reverse gear, Jet Girl and the Rippers just scythed them down. The Rippers did fight well in those days. Hard to believe it now, I know, seeing them all slumped in a drunken pile over there, dribbling and snoring, but they've degenerated a lot in the past few years. Too much late-night drinking and partying. And, of course, they can't get the batteries for their superhero body armour any more. But, back then, they were tough.

'Between them they took out the whole section of the base, including the administrative area where Sergeant Small was in command – I never did do the Sergeant Small penis jokes, did I? Never mind. But he was rumoured to have a really small penis. Anyway, this was when things went a little wrong. Someone had miscalculated.'

'You had,' says Jet Girl.

'I *knew* you were going to say that,' says Tank Girl.

'Well, you had.'

'It wasn't just me. You and the Rippers helped plan the raid.'

'But you were in charge.'

'That's not the point. A general must at some time rely on information provided by her intelligence services. If Donner got us a load of crap information with his scanner, it wasn't my fault. Was that thing he had really a radar screen? I'm convinced he only used it to watch videos of *The Simpsons*. Anyway, never mind whose fault it was, a miscalculation arose. The base was bigger than we thought it was. Despite Jet Girl and the Rippers successfully wiping out the troops in an entire section, there turned out to be a lot more sections than we'd bargained for. Thousands more troops arrived, advancing behind tanks and mobile guns, and things were looking bleak. Jet Girl and the kangaroos were trapped.'

I win the hand. Tank Girl and Sub Girl drink. Sub Girl's eyes close and she slowly slides off her chair. Ootsie catches her and prevents her from falling to the floor. One way of getting your loved one into your arms, I suppose.

At this, a great shout goes up from the crowd.

'Sub Girl is out of the game. She's passed out! Now it's just Tank Girl and the Trader!'

Tank Girl has a good laugh at the fate of Sub Girl, looking on with amusement as Ootsie and Jet Girl gently carry her away.

'Poor old Subby. Couldn't take it. Just you and me left, Trader. May the best woman win.'

'Or the best man,' I counter.

'Don't make me laugh,' says Tank Girl.

30

In the brief interval caused by Sub Girl's demise, Bitsy worms his way through the crowd and squeezes in beside me.

'Trader,' he says, eagerly. 'Who is that Goddess in the green head-dress?'

I groan.

'Bitsy, surely you haven't fallen in love again already? It's only five minutes since you were in love with Tank Girl.'

Bitsy growls.

'Kindly do not mention the loathsome Tank Girl in the same breath as the angel in green warpaint. Who is she?'

'Iris Grim.'

Bitsy looks rapturous.

'Iris Grim? What a divine name. Like the sound of water trickling gently through the meadows.'

Well, as Iris Grim is usually to be found roaring around on a huge motorbike with a sawn-off shotgun and a six-pack of beer, I cannot see that this is a very appropriate metaphor, but I let it pass.

'Bitsy, don't fall in love with Iris Grim. She'll only cause you more misery. Why do you keep falling for these totally inappropriate women?'

Bitsy looks displeased.

'I do not "keep falling for" anyone. I may have had slight, boyish attachments before, but this is the real thing. I love her. Look at her head-dress. Isn't it magnificent?'

And with this he departs, heading in the direction of the Post-Apocalypse Biker Girls.

Tank Girl complains that she is bored.

'Stop telling your life history,' I suggest.

She swears at me.

'I mean I'm bored with the game, Trader. And bored with sitting next to you. Forty-six hours of your company is more than enough for anyone. How about upping the stakes and getting it over with?'

I am still completely enfogged with alcohol and weariness and can't work out if this would be to my advantage or not. Tank Girl has a vast pile of money in front of her, far greater than my modest amount. If we raise the stakes it might give me a chance to catch up more quickly. There again, it might just lose me everything I have in the next few hands.

I am normally a cautious man. Slow perseverance is my forte. On the other hand, I am keenly aware that the longer I sit here in Big Mary's Bar and Grill, the more likely it is that everyone I've sold the *Venus de Milo* to will find out about everyone else I've sold it to, and there will be terrible trouble. If I have to disappear like lightning out of the door and into the newly super-charged Big Trader Truck, I want to have at least finished the game first. Also, I still have confidence that the palm-tree vodka will get to Tank Girl eventually. After all, it saw Sub Girl off soon enough. Even now Tank Girl is yawning. In fact, all of a sudden, she is looking pretty much out of it. Her eyes seem to be rotating in their sockets. I believe she may be on her way out. I agree to raise the stakes.

Tank Girl grins, immediately alert.

'Fine, sucker. Ante up and let's get going. Your deal.'

I try to shuffle the cards, but I find it almost as difficult as Sub Girl did. My fingers feel like big bananas. I drop a few cards on to the floor. Having no lovestruck companion like Ootsie to pick them up for me, I spend a long time fumbling around under the table. Coming back up I bang my head and everything goes dark for a few seconds. I groan.

'Good comedy routine,' says Tank Girl, bleakly unsympathetic. 'Now get on with it.'

'Come on, Trader, concentrate,' says an encouraging voice at my side. It is the Professor. He's woken up and made his way back to the table. Good, the Professor's friendly presence is encouraging, even if he does look rather the worse for wear.

I deal. Tank Girl resumes her narrative.

'So, there were Jet Girl and the Rippers trapped in the middle of a large army. And, you may remember, I was meanwhile hanging desperately on to a swaying bridge –'

'*Pons asinorum*,' mutters the Professor.

'What?' demands Tank Girl.

'Nothing,' says the Professor, which is just as well, as he tells me later that it is Latin for "Asses bridge".

'As I was saying, I was hanging desperately on, with Kesslee about to cut the last remaining cable, sending me lunging to my doom thousands of feet below.'

'It wasn't thousands of feet,' sniffs Jet Girl.

'How the hell would you know?' demands Tank Girl. 'You weren't there.'

'The administration block was only three stories high,' says Jet Girl.

'Jet Girl, will you just shut the fuck up? Stop this constant interrupting. What a pain you are sometimes.

Okay, it wasn't thousands of feet, it was only three stories. Three big stories, though. It was a fuck of a long way down, I can tell you. You think it's any fun falling three stories on to concrete?'

'I'm just trying to keep the story accurate,' says Jet Girl.

Tank Girl gives her a really evil glare. Unfortunately for Tank Girl, this coincides with her playing a king on a king and I call *snap!* Tank Girl transfers her baleful gaze briefly to me before turning again to Jet Girl.

'Now see what you've done! You made me lose the hand! How am I meant to concentrate when you keep contradicting me and arguing about irrelevancies? Kindly keep quiet while I tell my story and beat the Trader here. Honestly, Jet Girl, after all I've done for you – the amount of times I've saved your life, not to mention helping you through personal crises and teaching you how to drink – you might show me a bit more regard. Now stop trying to sabotage everything.'

I'm pleased at this show of hostility between my rivals, but once more I feel sorry for Jet Girl. Such a pleasant young woman.

Tank Girl slams one motorbike boot on to the table, gets her head down and deals the cards with a great show of concentration. This concentration only lasts a few seconds, however. Incapable of keeping quiet for any length of time, she swiftly resumes her tale.

'There I was, swaying about hundreds of feet in the air, with Kesslee revving up his cyber-arm and heading for the last steel rope. With one swipe, he sliced right through it. I had only a fraction of a second to act. I took a mighty leap off the plummeting lump of metal and caught hold of the cable with one hand. Supremely

151

athletic. But my problems weren't over. I was going up that cable like a rat up a drainpipe, trying to reach safety before Kesslee cut it as well. It was close: I was nearly at the top, but just before I reached it Kesslee sliced the cable through. He gave me this sneering grin and shouted "farewell Tank Girl" but he hadn't counted on my aforementioned superb athleticism. I leapt from the cable and got my hand on his ankle. We swayed around on the ledge for a few seconds before toppling over. And there we were, locked in a vicious embrace, plunging towards the ground far below.

'Was this the end for Tank Girl? *Snap!*'

Tank Girl wins the hand.

'It looked like it might be. But I twisted desperately in mid air, struggled free of Kesslee, got one hand on to a flag-pole that was sticking out the wall, did a complete rotation and launched myself over the gap, where I caught on to a window ledge with my fingernails. *Snap!*'

Tank Girl wins the hand.

'I stayed there for about half a second before the wood started to give way. I was still hundreds of feet above the ground and once more plunging to my doom. There were no more flag-poles anywhere convenient so, thinking quickly, I took off my belt and threw it like a lasso towards a small nail that was sticking out the wall. It caught, and I hung there – bruised, battered but still alive. *Snap!*'

Tank Girl wins the hand.

'I dropped down lightly to the ground, expecting to find Kesslee splattered in a heap somewhere nearby, but, to my total disgust, I saw that he'd managed to ram his cyber-arm into the wall about halfway up and then let himself down gently. There was a big groove right the way down the wall where he'd made his descent. We didn't waste any time congratulating each other on our survival but leapt straight into another savage battle. *Snap!*'

Tank Girl wins the hand.

'We fought this way and that, Kesslee with his deadly arm and me just with my bare hands and feet. Completely brutal combat. Kesslee got me a few times and there was blood everywhere, but on his next attack I ducked under his arm and gave him a stomping kick right in the guts. He flew into the air and landed on a fence. *Snap!*'

Tank Girl wins the hand. She laughs.

'It turned out to be an electric fence. Kesslee was trapped there by his cyber-arm and you could see the electricity surging through it jerking him around like a puppet. Most amusing thing that happened all day. But I have to hand it to him, Kesslee was tough. It didn't kill him. He wrenched himself free and came at me again. He was looking hurt, though, and his arm didn't seem to be working properly any more, so I was just thinking that this would be a good opportunity to mangle him once and for all when you know what happened? *Snap!*'

Tank Girl wins the hand.

'He flicked a switch on his arm and a rocket came out. Imagine! A small anti-personnel rocket concealed there all the time. Well, I tried getting out of the way, but by this time I was a mass of cuts, bruises, sprains, contusions and broken limbs, and definitely *not* the lithe and agile Tank Girl you all know today. I leapt back and managed to avoid the rocket, but it exploded on the wall beside me and I was knocked senseless by a pile of bricks and assorted debris falling on my head. *Snap!*'

Tank Girl wins the hand.

'When I opened my eyes, Kesslee was standing over me, cyber-arm pointing at my throat. I was trapped. I couldn't move. This was the end. *Snap!*'

Tank Girl wins the hand.

Big Mary announces a break.

'We don't need one,' says Tank Girl. 'The Trader's run out of money. He's lost. I win.'

31

I have indeed run out of money. Disaster looms. Disaster has arrived, in fact.

'Wait,' I say, as Tank Girl commences crowing about her victory. 'I'm not out of it yet.'

'You've got no money.'

'But I haven't passed out. And Big Mary just declared a break. Normal custom and practice says, if I can raise a stake before the break's over, then I'm still in.'

'Is that right?' demands the hideous Tank Female, looking over at Big Mary, who commonly acts as referee on all dubious matters.

'Suppose so,' replies Big Mary.

'God, I'm bored with this,' says Tank Girl. 'Anyway, where are you going to get money?'

'I have my methods,' I reply, and depart swiftly, or as swiftly as I can through the throng. As I struggle past I can feel the eyes of the Children of the Temple of the Sun staring at me like buzzards waiting for breakfast; may they all trip over their tacky yellow robes and break their collective necks.

The crowd is thinner at the far end of the bar. Sitting at a table surrounded by Loretta Dragon Slayer, the Four Dwarfs and various minions of evil appearance, is John the Brute, Bandit King of the Red Mountains, as I may already have mentioned. Being rather drunk, I almost give him a friendly pat on the shoulder but am prevented from doing so by a murderous stare from Loretta Dragon Slayer, who is cleaning her nails with a large samurai sword. Never mind, I shoot him a hearty greeting, anyway.

'John the Brute, esteemed Bandit King, how good of you to wait. I am sorry to have kept you so long, but you know how it is when playing with scum like these. I have to keep them in their place.'

'We heard you lost the game, Trader.'

'Absolutely not. Just a normal break in the proceedings. When it's over, I'm going to clean Tank Girl out. Show her who's boss. Seeing as you detest Tank Girl, I expect you'll be glad to show your appreciation towards me . . . which brings me neatly on to the main subject, the *Venus de Milo*.'

'How much?' says John the Brute, never one for small-talk.

'Well, it *is* an item of quite astonishing rarity. The *Venus de Milo*. Discovered by the French Admiral Dumond d'Urville on Milo, one of the Greek Islands that existed before the comet struck, raising the sea and causing earthquakes and general havoc everywhere. Sometimes called Melos. Made around the second century BC. Long regarded as the finest work of ancient art still extant. Quite an item.'

The Professor told me all this earlier. A man of quite astonishing erudition, the Professor.

'100 zoobies,' says John the Brute.

I chuckle.

'Really, John. The museum in Lugit would pay 1,000,000 zoobies at least.'

'You're not in Lugit City. You're in Big Mary's Bar and Grill, and you're talking to a man who already doesn't like you. 100 zoobies.'

'50,000.'

'I'll give you 120 zoobies.'

'I can't go lower than 45,000.'

John the Brute rises from his chair. He towers over me in a most alarming way.

'You don't seem to quite understand, Trader. I haven't come here to haggle with you. I've come here to take the statue as a present for Juliet. I'm only giving you the 120 because I'm in a good mood after a bottle of rum. So, I suggest you take it and go . . . unless you want to be tied to the wheel of my armoured car and driven over the desert back to the Red Mountains.'

Well, really. I am outraged. This is just shocking. Who does this thug think he is, muscling in on my territory and trying to make off with such a priceless item for a measly 120 zoobies?

Who he thinks he is, I suppose, is a fantastically strong, violent and psychopathic robber with a big gang of friends with him. Difficult for me to argue when it comes right down to it.

John the Brute stands glowering at me. The scars on his neck and forehead stand out clearly. His long, dirty yellow hair flows over his shoulders like that of a Viking of old. On his back he has three machetes. Behind him, the dwarfs are sniggering at my discomfiture. John the Brute nods to one of his henchmen, who comes forward and gives me a small purse of money. A very small purse.

'Where is the statue?'

'I must protest very strongly about this. I am highly dubious about the legality of –'

Loretta Dragon Slayer leaves her chair so quickly that I hardly see a thing until she is standing behind me with her sword at my throat.

'It's on a chair over in the corner,' I tell them. 'Wearing a baseball cap and a combat jacket. You can't miss her, she's got no arms.'

I am defeated. Thugs. Criminals. I detest them. They are taking my 1,000,000-zoobie statue and giving me 120 zoobies. Not even enough to pay off ZugZug, or any of the people I have taken money from for the statue. Hardly enough for a few more hands of cards.

I trudge sadly through the crowd back to the table. I have one small spark of hope, which is that I might still win the game.

Tank Girl quickly extinguishes it by bursting out laughing when I put my 120 zoobies on the table. She has thousands in front of her.

'Is that it, Trader? That's all you could raise? Well, that should keep you going for another few minutes if you're lucky. Hey, Jet Girl, go and get the beers in, it'll be time to celebrate soon.'

Tank Girl leans over to whisper in my ear.

'Are you feeling strange, Trader?'

'Huh? What do you mean?'

'Strange. Perhaps overly affected by alcohol. Like maybe you've drunk a glass of beer liberally laced with Big Mary's lethal palm-tree vodka . . .?'

I stare at her. She stares back at me. We have a good stare at each other.

'I switched the glasses,' she says. 'While you were fumbling under the table for the cards. I have an unusually fine nose for alcohol, you know. I guessed what you'd done. How are you feeling?'

A little weak, now she mentions it. Imagining the deadly concoction circulating inside me, I quickly start to feel weaker. It is funny how many things can all go wrong in such a short space of time.

'My deal, I believe.'

Tank Girl grabs the cards. She is unbearably pleased with herself. I know she is going to finish off her story. She does. I hate her.

32

Very slowly I push my stake into the centre of the table. With the raised amounts we are now playing for I can last for only four hands without a win. Given the way Tank Girl triumphed in every one of the last series of games, I cannot muster any confidence in my chances.

I try and picture what is going to happen when I lose. ZugZug will immediately demand her 500 zoobies and set the Children of the Temple of the Sun on me when I am unable to produce it. John the Brute will take the statue away only to find he is in competition for it with the Wasteland Ninjas, the Shaolin Queens and the Post-Apocalypse Biker Girls. And the Post-Apocalypse Biker Boys? Did I sell it to Marlin as well? Possibly – my memory is hazy on a few parts of the last couple of days.

None of these people are going to be very pleased with me. Already I can see Eldrich San, Magdalen and Iris Grim closing in on the statue, each one thinking that it is theirs to take away. They may find it hard to understand why exactly I have sold it to all of them and cannot refund the money. The words 'thief', 'criminal' and 'kill him' may spring to mind. The honest and well-respected Trader is soon going to be the most unpopular man this side of the Red Mountains.

Yes, there's no getting away from it, I am in terrible trouble. As for my plan to flee immediately to the Big Trader Truck waiting outside, I find that, after drinking the palm-tree vodka, my legs no longer work.

A barman brings over a tray with an order of milk and aspirin for the Professor.

'Keep going, Trader, you're not out of it yet.'

'Thank you, Professor. How are you feeling?'

'Terrible. I woke with a dreadful headache.'

'Shouldn't you go home and get some sleep?'

The Professor shrugs.

> '"*Meum est propositum in taberna mori;*
> *Ubi vinum proximum morientis ori*
> *Tunc cantabunt laetius angelorum chori;*
> *Deus sit propitius huic potatori.*"'

'Eh, pardon Professor?'

> '"It is my intention to die in a tavern;
> May wine be placed to my dying lips,
> That when the choirs of angels shall come they
>   may say;
> God be merciful to this drinker."

It's an old drinking song.'

'Bit morbid, isn't it?'

'It sounds rather more jolly sung in Latin.'

I nod vaguely, but I doubt if any song about dying in a tavern would sound particularly jolly to me right now.

'Okay, cut out the chatter and pay attention,' roars the horrible Tank Beast. 'Last round of the game coming up.'

Everyone cheers.

'During which, I will fill you in on the rest of the story, which had reached a pretty exciting, nay, thrilling climax, with Jet Girl surrounded by troops and me trapped under rubble with Kesslee about to cut my throat. And all the time Sam's voice was coming over the tannoy begging for help and saying that the water was getting higher and higher and she was about to drown and was too young to die. It was very sad. In other circumstances I might possibly have wept. However, as I was at that moment trapped under a pile of bricks and Kesslee was aiming a deadly blow at my throat, I had other things on my mind. As he drew back his arm I let out a piercing whistle.'

'"Your death cry, Tank Girl?" said Kesslee.

'"No," I replied, "I'm calling for my tank."

'He laughed. Foolish of him, really, because right then my tank trundled round the corner and knocked him senseless. Yep, the trusty old tank had come to the rescue, responding to my whistle in the nick of time. It batted Kesslee away with its gun turret, then proceeded to dig me out of the rubble. Never has a young lady been more grateful to her tank.

'Kesslee was stunned. He lay on the ground dazed, while I clambered into the trusty war-machine. I was bruised, battered and aching beyond all human endurance, but, naturally, my endurance is greater than your average human's. I seem to remember I actually whistled a happy tune as I aimed the powerful gun at Kesslee, ready to blow him off the face of the earth.

'"Fire!" I yelled. Did I mention that my tank is voice-sensitive? Well, it is. Responds to my every command. It's a really terrific tank. Unfortunately nothing happened.

'"Fire!" I yelled again. "Hey, what's going on? Why aren't you firing?" A sign flashed up on the control panel. Out of ammunition. The tank had used up all its shells carrying out its heroic attack on the base.

'"You silly tank," I said. "Couldn't you have saved

just one?" Now Kesslee was starting to stir. I really did not want to go and fight him again. I was bored with it. Besides, I had to end it quickly if I was still to rescue Sam, now presumably in some difficulties in the pipe. So, in a moment of glorious inspiration, I started gathering up all the empty beer cans in the tank, of which there were a great many, and ramming them into the gun chamber.

'"This'll do it," I muttered, and crammed them in till it was full. Kesslee stood up. He activated his cyber-arm and started advancing towards me, hatred and murder in his eyes. "Fire!" I yelled, and the tank blasted him with a lethal fusillade of crushed beer cans. The effect was spectacular. Cut him to ribbons. Bits of Kesslee flew everywhere. Most satisfying. "Good tank," I said, and gave it a kiss. I do love my tank.

'So that was it for my part of the battle. Kesslee was defeated, and I was off to rescue Sam.'

Beside me I hear the Professor muttering that that was the single most ridiculous story he had ever heard, and I can only agree. She shot him with beer cans? And, oh yeah, the beer cans just happened to fit into the gun barrel. Didn't jam up the mechanism or anything. Never mind. I've lost one round. Three more to go.

As Tank Girl nears the climax of her story, she is shouting, yelling and waving her arms around. The audience respond, cheering and clapping. On stage Alvin's band breaks into another number and the Sex Pistols' fuzzbox makes the music scream and wail. Tank Girl shouts even louder. So does everyone else. Beside me the Professor is muttering about Dante. I'm finding it all fairly hellish myself.

163

'Tank Girl wins again! Kesslee beaten, I sprinted off to find Little Wee Sam, my tank following faithfully behind. Now, Jet Girl, remember, due to some miscalculations on her part, was finding life difficult. She and the Rippers had managed to defeat the first thousand or so troops, destroy their tanks and aircraft and so on, but thousands more now had them surrounded and were lobbing shells, grenades, kitchen furniture and whatever else came to hand. They were sheltering under a burnt-out truck wondering what to do, when, suddenly, the ground started to shake. It cracked and rumbled, and the earth churned, bringing buildings crashing down all around them. Huge crevasses opened up, swallowing entire divisions of enemy soldiers and causing panic and chaos in the ranks.

'From the epicentre of this earthquake an amazing sight appeared – it was Sub Girl in her newly completed giant underground submarine! *Snap!* That's another hand to me, I believe!

'Sub Girl had saved the day. The enemy fell back in confusion as Sub Girl's massive construction churned its way above ground, guns blazing in all directions. It was enormous, a vast behemoth, an unstoppable fighting machine spewing fire and brimstone in all directions!'

The Professor looks very dubious about all this.

'Is this the submarine she was making in her workshop?'

'That's right.'

'The workshop she used to disguise as a restaurant during the day?'

'That's right.'

'Was this restaurant by any chance the size of an

aircraft hangar and equipped with a vast array of ship-building equipment?'

'No, it wasn't, smart-ass,' says Tank Girl, impatient at the interruption. 'It was a small restaurant. The workshop at the back only had a blowtorch and a couple of benches. It just so happens that Sub Girl is an unusually gifted mechanic and was able to run up a complex and gigantic piece of machinery using only primitive tools. Never underestimate the power of a determined woman.

'Now, as I was saying, the submarine came to rest above ground, guns blazing away in all directions. And while those troops that hadn't tumbled down into giant crevasses were trying to regroup, Sub Girl shot off the doors to the slave pens. A very smart move, couldn't have done better myself. Thousands of miserable prisoners held captive by Water and Power rushed out into the fray, waving sticks. The troops were terrified. This was too much for them. Their lines wavered. When word came over the tannoy that Tank Girl had killed Kesslee and was now heading their way looking mean, they broke and fled.

'Meanwhile, I had located Sam and hauled her out of the water-pipe, completely unharmed. Apart from the psychological trauma that led to her becoming an alcoholic at the age of eleven and wandering around the desert moaning "why didn't they rescue me earlier?" but, hey, she might have turned out bad, anyway. She's been showing some signs of improving recently.

'So that was that. Total victory to us. The most famous victory in the history of the world, I would say. The vast Water and Power military industrial conglomerate overthrown by Sub Girl, Jet Girl and eight kangaroos, led by me, Field Marshal Tank Girl. Stupendous, I call it. Since then, the world has been free. Yes, it would be difficult to put into words just how much everybody in this room owes me. *Snap!* I do declare. You've got one game left, Trader. Enjoy it.'

33

ZugZug the Bookmaker sits right down at the table, balancing on the edge of Magdalen's seat. Magdalen does not seem to mind. No doubt she has bet heavily on Tank Girl, curse her red topknot. As I am now struggling desperately to remain in the game, this is the very last thing I need. It would be easier to concentrate with a buzzard in full funeral dress perched on my shoulder.

All I have left in front of me is enough money for one more game. People are already screaming in praise of Tank Girl's victory. The pressure on me is unbearable.

On the positive side, feeling starts to return to my legs, driven there, no doubt, by fear and adrenalin. Would sudden flight to the Big Trader Truck still be possible? I wonder.

'We're watching the truck,' says ZugZug. She must be psychic. That seems very unfair, what with her being a bookmaker and everything. It has to be unethical.

It is my deal. As I shuffle, Bitsy suddenly appears and whispers to me, 'Trader, you have to put in a good word for me with Iris Grim. She's ignoring me.'

'Are you out of your mind?' I scream, and push him away. I'm always willing to help a young lover, you understand, but not right at this moment.

Tank Girl calls out to Grid the Barman and he pushes his way over, balancing a tray on his arm. On the tray is a bottle of Big Mary's palm-tree vodka, special reserve extra strength. As drunk only by those tired of life.

Tank Girl, who is not tired of life, picks it up and takes a huge slug out of bravado. She smacks her lips and slams the bottle down on the table.

The crowd goes wild.

'Please keep that stuff away from me,' says Sub Girl, who has reappeared, shaky, but just about in control. She is helped into her seat by Ootsie.

'Sub Girl!' cries Tank Girl. 'My old friend! You're back. You missed the terrific build-up I gave you in my story, but you're just in time to see me win the game. Deal the cards, Trader.'

I deal. We play. The cards go: five, ten, king, queen, three, two, nine, ten, ace, four, jack and so on, for a long time. The noise in the bar gradually dies away as the game goes round. For the first time since entering Big Mary's, even Tank Girl manages to be quiet.

Eight, four, king, ace, two, ace, nine, jack, seven, four, eight, king, they go on. I can't bear it. The adrenalin is now pumping wildly through my body, so that I'm shaking in my chair and banging each card down almost out of control. Sometimes I practically miss the table.

Nine, queen, six, three, jack, two, six, five, five –

'*SNAP!!!*'

I thrust out my arm. So does Tank Girl. Our hands thud down on to the table, and we wrestle for control.

'Mine, mine!' I scream.

'I was first! It's mine!' screams Tank Girl.

There is confusion; then, a hush. Big Mary leans over us, inspecting the scene.

'Tank Girl's hand was down first,' she says. 'Game to her.'

Chaos breaks out in the bar. Jet Girl, Sub Girl and

various other creeps and sycophants are dragging Tank Girl up to cheer her round the bar, cans of beer are cracking open and flying everywhere, when, suddenly, a gunshot breaks through the commotion. People pause, some looking round questioningly, some diving for cover. Bizarrely, the man holding the gun turns out to be the Professor, who has lifted it from Big Mary's apron. Having fired a shot in the air to get everyone's attention, he is now dragging the *Venus de Milo* from it's chair.

'Help me with this,' he says, and a nearby Biker Girl gives him a hand to lift it on to the card-table.

'Game not over,' he states. 'The Trader still has this. He bets a 1,000,000-zoobie statue against all Tank Girl's winnings.'

'Yes, yes!' scream the various voices of those around the table wishing further excitement.

'No, no!' scream various others, presumably those who think the statue already belongs to them.

I do not know what to make of this. I can see the Professor is trying to help me, but whether he actually *is* helping or not, I can't tell. For the moment I am beyond thinking. Before I can clear my head, and before anyone else can do anything about it, Tank Girl settles the matter by bellowing with laughter and shouting that, yes, she agrees to the bet. The Professor has successfully appealed to her bravado and self-esteem. And possibly her stupidity. And possibly the prospect of netting 1,000,000 zoobies. Who knows with Tank Girl?

'That's the way I like things,' she roars. 'Everything on one turn of the cards. Tank Girl never refuses a challenge. Give me those cards!'

She grabs the pack, brushing aside some protests from Magdalen, shuffles them rapidly, and deals.

Knowing that there is no time to lose before John the Brute or some other thug protests violently about the way things are going, I play my first card immediately. Tank Girl replies and we thrust the cards down one after the other at the fastest possible pace. The game lasts for three seconds. The cards come out: five, three, king, eight, king, queen, two, two –

'*SNAP!*'

This time, Tank Girl and I both fling our whole bodies on to the table. Tank Girl, naturally, is fitter, stronger, quicker and more alert than me, but I am made completely desperate by my situation. I fling myself at the pair of twos like a madman and somewhere around the base of the *Venus de Milo* I collide bodily with Tank Girl who is flinging herself in the same direction with equal enthusiasm.

The table cannot take the weight of two bodies and an ancient statue. They are just rubbish, these tables in Big Mary's. It splits apart and we crash on to the floor, both of us all the while screaming, 'It's mine, I won, I was first', for all we're worth.

We land in a tangled heap on the ground, and the chaos that now erupts makes all previous outbreaks of chaos in Big Mary's seem genteel by comparison. Tank Girl and I are struggling furiously on the floor, each trying to simultaneously hold on to the pair of twos and the *Venus de Milo*, but as we are, in fact, rolling about on top of the still-slumbering Sam, it's hard to get a proper grip. Voices nearby are raised in fury, and I recognize Magdalen's screaming that the statue is hers, *she* bought it. Iris Grim is shouting much the same and they both start calling their gangs to arms. Eldrich San and the Wasteland Ninjas fight their way through to the centre of the scene, where they stake their claim in a loud and determined manner. Instantly comes the sound of the Biker Boys doing exactly the same and in no time the four gangs are screaming abuse at each other and drawing weapons.

'Damn you all, the statue's mine, the Trader owes it to me,' yells the utterly venal ZugZug. 'To me, Children of the Temple of the Sun. Form up and attack.'

Although I am still engaged in desperate struggle with Tank Girl on the floor, I am not surprised when an excessively loud and hostile voice is raised above the clamour.

'Get back, you maggots!' roars John the Brute. 'The *Venus de Milo* is mine! Dwarfs! Loretta! Forward!'

Down on the floor with me, Tank Girl stops struggling, though without loosening her grip on the statue.

'Trader,' she says. 'What *have* you been up to?'

34

Another gunshot rings out, followed by Big Mary's thunderous voice: 'We'll have no trouble in my bar!'

She'll be lucky.

The gunshot into the ceiling and Big Mary's imposing presence do at least serve to postpone the inevitable hostilities. The huge figure of Big Mary, gun in hand, is an intimidating sight.

Magdalen, however, is not intimidated. With the rest of the Shaolin Queens behind her, she tells Mary to get out of her way because the *Venus de Milo* belongs to them and they are taking it away right now.

'You are not, you Shaolin pigs,' cries Iris Grim. 'The statue belongs to the Post-Apocalypse Biker Girls. We bought it from the trader.'

'You're lying!'

'Oh yeah?'

'What is the meaning of this?' demands Eldrich San, sounding like an outraged schoolmaster. 'The *Venus de Milo* belongs to neither of your pathetic gangs. It is the property of the Wasteland Ninjas. The Trader sold it to us.'

I think they might all be looking at me at this point, but I can't really see. I'm too busy trying to hide under Tank Girl.

'They are a bunch of thieving swines, all of them,' yells Marlin, smashing his fist on a table and breaking it in two.

'Mind my tables,' protests Big Mary.

'To hell with your tables. The statue belongs to the Biker Boys. We bought it.'

Behind him, the entire ranks of the Post-Apocalypse Biker Boys draw up threateningly. I suppose I must have sold it to them as well. I really can't remember doing that.

'But I bought it,' wails Ootsie. 'It was a present for –.' Seeing the assembled violent hordes around him and the terrifying stare Eldrich San gives him, he thinks better of this and falls silent.

There is movement in the crowd.

'It is mine. I bought it. It is a present for Juliet, Bandit Queen of the Red Mountains,' says John the Brute, appearing centre-stage. He is flanked by Loretta Dragon Slayer and the Four Dwarfs.

'And we're taking it back to the Red Mountains. Wrapped up in the remains of the Trader.'

There seems to be no widespread protest about this last part.

The gangs stare with hatred at each other. Those people in the audience not directly involved withdraw to the safety of the far corners. Many people, deciding that it is better to be wet than dead, depart the premises. Big Mary still holds her gun but she can tell it is useless. Nothing is going to stop the factions going to war.

Tank Girl leaps to her feet, depriving me of cover. I try and hide under Sam.

'Wait a minute. What's all this? Are you all out of your minds? The statue belongs to me. I won it fair and square.'

'I thought the Trader won it,' says the Professor, which is very brave of him in the circumstances.

'My hand was down first,' claims Tank Girl.

'But it shouldn't have been in the game at all,' protests Iris Grim. 'The statue was not the Trader's to stake. *I* bought it.' The green warpaint on her face seems to glow with anger.

'No, *I* bought it!' says practically everyone else in the room.

'Well, bollocks to you all,' says Tank Girl. 'The statue is mine. It's mine by right of conquest. It was in the treasure-room at Water and Power when I defeated Kesslee, and that means it's mine. I just left it there for safe-keeping. Doesn't mean the Trader had any right to remove it.'

Here everyone looks at me again, but I just have nothing to say.

'So, it was mine all along,' continues Tank Girl. 'And anyone that wants it is going to have to take it off me.'

At this, both Sub Girl and Jet Girl rise unsteadily from their places and stand beside Tank Girl.

John the Brute takes a pace forward.

'Tank Girl,' he says. 'I am going to kill you.'

Of all the factions in the Bar and Grill, possibly excluding Tank Girl's, John the Brute's is surely the strongest. But, either because he wants to leave nothing to chance, or maybe just because he doesn't want them getting in the way, he makes an appeal to the others. He motions to one of his subordinates, and five bags are produced. He tosses one to Magdalen, one to Marlin, one to Iris Grim, one to ZugZug and one to Eldrich San.

'5000 zoobies each,' he says. 'I take the statue and I pay you for your help.'

Everyone looks at Tank Girl to see what she will do. Will she appeal to her friendship with some of the gangs? Will she make out a strong case for the statue really being hers and try to use persuasion? Will she proffer an alternative bribe?

'Bollocks to you all, you scumbags,' says Tank Girl defiantly, and spits on the floor. 'The statue's mine.'

And so began the greatest fight ever seen in the Wastelands, in which Tank Girl, Jet Girl and Sub Girl took on the combined forces of John the Brute, Loretta Dragon Slayer, the Four Dwarfs, The Post-Apocalypse Biker Girls, the Post-Apocalypse Biker Boys, the Shaolin Queens of the Desert, the Wasteland Ninjas and the Children of the Temple of the Sun.

35

As the assembled forces face each other, Big Mary and her bar-staff take the only sensible course of action open to them and hide behind the bar. Tank Girl, Jet Girl and Sub Girl are close to me in the corner. Over the other side of the room are the massed gangs. To my great misfortune, they are between me and the door. I can tell that it is going to be no use hiding beneath Sam as she is much too small to provide any decent cover, so I leave her where she lies and crawl toward a table, hoping that no one notices me. Where the Professor has got to, I do not know.

I have just reached the furthermost table and secreted myself underneath it when the fight begins. I mutter a prayer for my safety and turn round to see what is happening. Tank Girl is standing with her back to the wall, baseball bat in hand, her mouth set in a grim line. Her face paint has melted down her cheeks in a series of ugly black streaks. On her left is Jet Girl, and on her right, Sub Girl. Their enemies are charging down the room shrieking war-cries and brandishing a huge variety of blunt and sharp instruments.

As the wave of assailants breaks over them, I cringe. Jet Girl disappears beneath a pile of Biker Boys and Shaolin Queens, while Sub Girl is submerged by Biker Girls and Ninjas. Meanwhile, the Four Dwarfs and the Children of the Temple encircle Tank Girl and attempt to hack her down with axes, knives and broken bottles.

It is a terrible scene. Hugely outnumbered, the three

women fight like Furies. Like Valkyries even. Jet Girl emerges from the scrimmage surrounding her and viciously sets about her opponents with a chair before disappearing again into the mêlée. Two Ninjas fly backwards, dealt savage blows from Sub Girl, and lie close to me in a heap, but Sub Girl, terribly outnumbered, also disappears again in the crowd.

Tank Girl is, meanwhile, locked in savage and desperate combat with the Four Dwarfs, who each aim sledgehammer axe-blows at her. Tank Girl parries each blow and deals out great damage with her baseball bat, and soon, two of the dwarfs and many yellow-robed Children are lying at her feet. The Children of the Temple of the Sun are very numerous, however, and, possibly encouraged by their chanting and religious fervour, rush forward, ignoring the blows from the baseball bat, and drag Tank Girl to the ground.

I feel a presence beside me. It is ZugZug, also taking cover under the table. Apparently she does not engage in this sort of warfare herself.

'This is all your doing,' she snarls.

I deny it vehemently.

'Not at all. They've all just drunk too much. I warned them it would only lead to trouble.'

I notice that Ootsie is hanging back, no doubt not wishing to inflict any damage on the woman he loves. Of Bitsy there is no sign.

Now Jet Girl is up on a chair raining bottles on her enemies, and Sub Girl has rallied and swings from a light fitting kicking Biker Girls in the head. With quite unbelievable strength and savagery, Tank Girl rises again from the floor, throwing opponents in all directions before grabbing an axe from one of the fallen dwarfs and proceeding to use it with great efficiency.

Everywhere people are screaming in pain and rage. I see Magdalen confront Jet Girl and land a terrific blow on her face, but Jet Girl stands up to her and kicks her to the ground. The battle now surges up the bar-room as Tank Girl, Jet Girl and Sub Girl fight their way out of the corner but, in doing so, they allow more opponents to pour in behind them, all kicking, hacking and stabbing for all they're worth.

Another newcomer crawls in beside me and ZugZug. It is Bitsy, clutching a bloody nose.

'She hit me when I tried to help,' he wails. 'She said I got in the way.' I presume he means Iris Grim. Another love affair comes to an end.

At this moment, two Children of the Temple of the Sun come flying through the air, sent on their trajectory by Tank Girl. They land on top of the table and it crashes round our heads leaving us dazed and confused, in a tangle of cracked limbs, splintered wood and yellow cloth.

A lot of table-splintering going on today, I reflect. Big Mary will be irate.

When I next risk a look, peering out from under a yellow robe, Tank Girl has got herself a little space. All four dwarfs are now lying motionless, along with many other of John the Brute's helpers and various Children of the Temple but Loretta Dragon Slayer has now entered the fray. Disdaining to join the general mêlée, she has waited till now before making any move. She strides down the room, sword in hand, and bows to Tank Girl.

'Asshole,' snarls Tank Girl, and leaps at her with her

baseball bat. Loretta does something very fast with her sword and Tank Girl keeps right on flying, ending up on the ground with a nasty gash on her shoulder. Her baseball bat has been cut in half. Undaunted, she leaps at Loretta again and tries to ram the half-baseball-bat right down her throat, but the Kung Fu champion of the continent calmly parries the blow and again strikes Tank Girl. An expression of incredible fury settles on Tank Girl's face and she discards the baseball bat, picks up one of the prostrate dwarfs and hurls him at Loretta.

Loretta Dragon Slayer, possibly never before attacked by an unconscious dwarf, is taken by surprise and reels backwards, where she is sucked into the middle of the fight going on between Sub Girl and seven Ninjas. More bodies flow in between, so the fight between Loretta Dragon Slayer and Tank Girl remains unresolved.

I notice something very interesting lying nearby. One of the bags containing 5000 zoobies that John the Brute threw to the gang leaders has spilled on to the floor and rolled close to our table. Not being one to miss such an opportunity even at a time like this, I cautiously reach out my hand for it. I can't quite reach. I stretch a little further. I still can't reach. I wriggle my body out a few inches, which, on reflection, is a silly thing to do in the midst of such a battle. A bottle thrown by one of the Biker Girls misses its intended target and hits me on the head. I just manage to get my fingers round the money bag before passing out.

36

I am unconscious for only a short while, denied the rest I deserve by the rapacious ZugZug attempting to prise the bag of money out of my rigid fingers.

'Get off, it's mine!' I cry, not quite aware of what is happening.

'It's mine!' insists ZugZug, and we struggle for control of it, whilst simultaneously crawling back under the table.

Things have changed in the time I have been unconscious. The combat has come almost to an end, leaving Jet Girl and Sub Girl still on their feet – cut, bruised and exhausted, but triumphant. Each of them stands on top of a pile of bodies.

Tank Girl is surrounded by a still larger pile of bodies. Even more cut and bruised than her friends, her face is a frightening mess of blood and black paint. And she is not yet triumphant. Walking slowly down the bar-room is John the Brute, who has not yet involved himself in the battle.

Not fair, really, coming in fresh to the affray when Tank Girl has just spent forty-seven hours drinking and then had to fight an impossible number of enemies. Still, life in the Wastelands is rarely fair.

John the Brute, long Viking hair now tied in a plait, and a machete in each hand, confronts Tank Girl. Eight feet tall, he towers over her.

'You piece of slime,' he says.

Probably for the first time in her life, Tank Girl does

not reply to an insult. She is too exhausted to speak and sucks in air in large painful gulps.

Jet Girl attempts to join her but instead falls to the floor, too weak to move further. Sub Girl makes to come over, but Tank Girl waves her back. In truth, Sub Girl, exhausted to the point of collapse, would not be much help.

John the Brute, Bandit King of the Red Mountains, flies at Tank Girl, and I am unable to properly describe the combat that now follows. Myself and ZugZug, sated with fighting as we are, can only look on in wonder at the truly unbelievable savagery of the contest. Big Mary pokes her head over the bar and hides again immediately, because debris is now flying in all directions as Tank Girl and John the Brute tear the place to pieces. Chairs disintegrate, walls collapse and the building shakes as they lay into each other.

Eventually, Tank Girl, fighting bare-handed, lands such a punch on the Bandit King that he flies across the room. He crashes into the bar, bringing it down in pieces around him and revealing the crouching Big Mary and her bar-staff, who now attempt to hide behind small pieces of wood. Among their number is the Professor.

'Bog-head,' grunts Tank Girl, finally managing an insult, though not a very good one. 'You're dead.'

'No,' retorts John the Brute, raising himself on one knee. 'You are.'

He raises one hand. To my astonishment a hatch opens in his forearm. Out of the hatch appears a small anti-personnel rocket.

'Kesslee!' roars Tank Girl.

'That's right,' replies her foe. 'Kesslee.'

I watch the next sequence of events in wonderment. Kesslee fires the rocket. Tank Girl leaps out of the way and it explodes behind her, knocking her flying. She lands and gets to her feet in one smooth roll, now clutching her spare baseball bat. As the next rocket is fired, she bats it out of the way, and that is the end for Kesslee, aka John the Brute, Bandit King of the Red Mountains. Before he can fire again, Tank Girl is on top of him, beating him to a pulp with the bat.

The battle is over. I feel ill. I'm glad I wasn't involved.

37

I'm sitting on the floor with the survivors of the battle. Around me are Tank Girl, Sub Girl and Jet Girl. Grid the Barman is bandaging them up. Big Mary is wandering round with a mop, bucket and power-drill, complaining bitterly about all the damage, but as I saw her sneak one of the 5,000-zoobie bags of money into her apron, she doesn't really have much to complain about.

All the gangs have departed, taking with them their wounded. Alvin and his band are still here, having survived the affray by crowding into the small cupboard behind the stage that serves as a dressing-room, and bolting the door. All their equipment is ruined, though. We are joined by some of the kangaroos, all severely hungover. They are full of apologies for sleeping through the fight, but from the way they're all clutching their heads and moaning about never drinking again, I can't see that they would have been much help. Sam is still lying drunk in exactly the same position. Apparently, this is not unusual.

Tank Girl, never satisfied, demands to be acknowledged as victor in the Annual Wasteland Snap and Drinking Competition. Not content with winning the most stunning victory in Wastelands history against overwhelming odds, she insists that her hand was down on the final card first.

I wearily concur. It's not worth arguing about. She is going to take the statue anyway. Besides, the bag containing 5,000 zoobies is tucked securely in my jacket.

Having successfully resisted ZugZug's attempt to prise it from my fingers, I have paid off the debts that remain to be collected and have still made a reasonable profit. As has ZugZug. I know she has another of the bags on her. The day will never come when ZugZug does not make a profit.

'Are you going to sell the *Venus de Milo* in Lugit City for 1,000,000 zoobies?' asks Jet Girl.

Tank Girl shrugs.

'Not right now, I kind of like it. It'll do to keep my coat on when I'm sunbathing on the tank.'

Ootsie and Bitsy crawl out from under a pile of unclaimed bodies.

'Let me do that,' says Ootsie immediately, and takes over the bandaging of Sub Girl's head. She does not protest. Maybe she's warming to him. At least his affections are constant, unlike the fickle Bitsy.

Bitsy sits down heavily beside me. I am about to offer him some sympathy about Iris Grim breaking his nose and then departing without a word of apology, but I notice he does not appear sad. He is instead looking dumb.

'What an attractive young man Alvin is,' he says to me quietly. 'Do you know if he has a regular boyfriend?'

I stare at him.

'Bitsy, you are completely mad. Look at all the disappointments you've had already. Why risk another hopeless love?'

Bitsy sniffs.

'What do you mean, another hopeless love? Those previous feelings were not love. Mere infantile attractions. Not to be compared with the deep affection I feel for Alvin. Nothing wrong with that is there?'

'I suppose not,' I say. 'Alvin's a very nice young man.'

He's also one of the most debauched people on the planet and most probably incapable of registering a true emotion for more than fifteen seconds, but I let it pass. Bitsy will just have to get on with it. He goes off muttering about leaving the Wasteland Ninjas, learning to play an instrument and going on the road with the band.

'So,' says the Professor to Tank Girl. 'How is it that John the Brute turned out to be Kesslee? I thought you'd killed him years ago.'

Personally, I do not care to know the answer to this, but you have to understand that the Professor is always seeking out knowledge.

Tank Girl shakes her head.

'I guess he must have escaped from Water and Power headquarters before undergoing extensive plastic surgery and moving to the Red Mountains.'

'You said you blew him to pieces with a barrage of crushed beer cans,' points out Jet Girl.

'So? There were lots of bodies being blown to pieces that day. You couldn't expect me to keep track of every single one, could you? What was I meant to do, fingerprint the remains? Anyway, it's finished now.'

Outside, the rain is becoming less heavy. Soon it will be over and the desert will bloom. I decide to leave. Best to head on over the hills with my bag of money while Tank Girl is still in a good mood. I would not wish to wait around until she remembers the unfortunate matter of the palm-tree vodka. I offer the Professor a lift, which he accepts.

As we leave Tank Girl is getting back into her stride,

calling for beer and pizza and bragging noisily about her victory.

'Unparalleled in the history of the world, I reckon. Tank Girl triumphant on all sides. Dazzling. Stupendous. Professor, you're a literary man, why don't you write it all down in a book? What an amazing story it would make.'

The Professor smiles.

'I have a reputation to maintain. It would take a great deal of money to persuade me to write your story, Tank Girl.'

As we head for the door, Tank Girl can still be heard boasting about her famous and fantastical exploits.

'*Vox et praeterea nihil,*' mutters the Professor. 'Empty words, signifying nothing.'

'Hey, Professor!'

We pause at the door.

'*Vox Puellae Testudinis vox Deae!*' yells Tank Girl.

We depart. I rev up the Big Trader Truck and pull out through the puddles of water, heading for Lugit City for a little peace and some profitable trading. On the horizon I can see a small strip of sunshine.

'What did that mean?' I ask after a while.

'The voice of Tank Girl is the voice of God,' replies the Professor.

'Meaning, I suppose, that what Tank Girl says goes, which it generally does.'